"You make it sound like I'm your cheating wife."

She sighed. "I didn't leave you. I left my job."

But she *had* left him, Mac thought. It hadn't felt like an employee walking out, but a betrayal.

"Same thing." His gaze fixed on her and for the first time, he noticed that she wore a tiny tank top and a silky pair of drawstring pants. Her feet were bare and her toenails were painted a soft blush pink. Her hair was long and loose over her shoulders, just skimming the tops of her breasts.

Mac took a breath and wondered where that flash of heat swamping him had come from. He'd been with Andi nearly every day for the past six years and he'd never reacted to her like this before. Sure, she was pretty, but she was his assistant. The one stable, organized, efficient woman in his life, and he'd never taken the time to notice that she was so much more than that.

Now it was all he could notice.

* * *

A Bride for the Boss is part of the series Texas Cattleman's Club: Lies and Lullabies— Baby secrets and a scheming sheikh rock Royal, Texas

Dear Reader,

Working on a continuity series is always a treat. First, I get to work with some wonderful writers and together we plot and plan and tweak our stories so that hopefully, they all mesh into a wonderful experience for you. Our readers.

And really, I think this edition of the Texas Cattleman's Club continuity is great. I had a terrific time with this story.

There's nothing more fun than writing about a clueless man who wises up in time to realize that the woman of his dreams has always been right there in front of him.

David "Mac" McCallum is focused on his work and looking out for his younger sister Violet. For years, Andrea "Andi" Beaumont has been Mac's executive assistant. She keeps his business and his life organized and running smoothly. So when she abruptly quits her job, Mac has to do everything he can to get her back.

I hope you enjoy *A Bride for the Boss* and please, stop by my Facebook page to let me know what you think!

Until next time, happy reading!

Maureen Child

MAUREEN CHILD

———

A BRIDE FOR THE BOSS

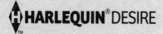

Special thanks and acknowledgment are given to Maureen Child for her contribution to the Texas Cattleman's Club: Lies and Lullabies miniseries.

Recycling programs for this product may not exist in your area

ISBN-13: 978-0-373-73463-4

A Bride for the Boss

Copyright © 2016 by Harlequin Books S.A.

This edition published by arrangement with Harlequin Books S.A.

For questions and comments about the quality of this book, please contact us at CustomerService@Harlequin.com.

Printed in U.S.A.

Maureen Child writes for the Harlequin Desire line and can't imagine a better job.

A seven-time finalist for a prestigious Romance Writers of America RITA® Award, Maureen is an author of more than one hundred romance novels. Her books regularly appear on bestseller lists and have won several awards, including a Prism Award, a National Readers' Choice Award, a Colorado Romance Writers Award of Excellence and a Golden Quill Award. She is a native Californian but has recently moved to the mountains of Utah.

Books by Maureen Child

Harlequin Desire

The Fiancée Caper
After Hours with Her Ex
Triple the Fun
Double the Trouble

Pregnant by the Boss

Having Her Boss's Baby
A Baby for the Boss
Snowbound with the Boss

Texas Cattleman's Club: Lies and Lullabies

A Bride for the Boss

Visit her Author Profile page at Harlequin.com, or maureenchild.com, for more titles.

To all of the wonderful writers in this fabulous continuity series—it's been an honor working with all of you.

And to Charles Griemsman, thanks for being such a great editor and for not tearing your hair out during this process!

One

"What do you mean, *you quit*?" David "Mac" McCallum stared at his assistant and shook his head. "If this is a joke, it's not funny."

Andrea Beaumont took a deep breath, then said sharply, "Not a joke, Mac. I'm dead serious."

He could see that, and he didn't much care for it. Usually when Andi stepped into his office, it was to remind him of a meeting or a phone call, or to tell him she'd come up with some new way to organize his life and business.

But at the moment, she had angry glints firing in her normally placid gray eyes, and he'd do well to pay attention. Having a younger sister had taught him early to watch his step around women. Violet had a temper that could peel paint, and Mac knew that a wise man stayed out of range when a woman got a certain look about her.

Right now, Andi—his calm, cool, organized executive assistant—appeared to be ready for battle.

Andi looked the same as always, even though she was in the middle of tossing his well-ordered world upside down. June sunlight slipped through the wide windows at Mac's back and poured over her like molten gold. Her long, straight, dark brown hair hung past the shoulders of the pale blue blazer she wore over a white dress shirt and dark blue jeans. Black boots, shined to a mirror gleam, finished off the outfit. Her storm-gray eyes were fixed on him unblinkingly and her full, generous mouth was pinched into a grim slash of determination.

Looked like they were about to have a "discussion."

Mac braced himself. Whatever she had in mind just wasn't going to fly. He couldn't afford to lose her. Hell, running McCallum Enterprises was a full-time job for ten men and damned if he'd let the woman who knew his business as well as he did simply walk away.

She'd been his right-hand man—woman—*person*— for the last six years and Mac couldn't imagine being without her. When something needed doing, Andi got it done. Mac didn't have to look over her shoulder, making sure things were handled. He could tell her what he needed and not worry about it. Andi had a knack for seeing a problem and figuring out the best way to take care of it.

She could smooth talk anyone, and if that didn't work, he'd seen her give an opponent a cool-eyed glare that could turn their blood cold. There'd been plenty of times when Mac had actually enjoyed watching her stare down an adversary. But he had to say, being on the receiving end of that icy look wasn't nearly as enjoyable.

What had brought this on?

"Why don't you take a seat and tell me what's got you so angry."

"I don't want a seat," she said. "And I don't want to be soothed like you do those horses you love so much..."

He frowned. "Then what exactly do you want?"

"I already told you. I want to quit."

"Why the hell would you want to do that?"

Her gray eyes went wide, as if she couldn't believe he even had to ask that question. But as far as Mac knew, everything was just as it should be. They'd closed the Donaldson deal the day before and now McCallum Enterprises could add Double D Energy Services to its ledgers. And Andi'd had a lot to do with getting David Donaldson to sign on the dotted line.

"I just gave you a raise last night for your work on the energy project."

"I know," she said. "And I earned it. That deal was not pretty."

"So what's the problem?"

"You told me to take over the planning for Violet's baby shower."

He drew his head back and narrowed his eyes on her in shocked surprise. With her talent for list making and organization, Andi should be able to handle that shower in a finger snap. "That's a problem? I thought you and Vi were friends."

"We *are*," she countered, throwing both hands high. "Of course we are. That's not the point."

"What *is* the point, then?" Mac dropped into his chair and, lifting his booted feet, crossed them at the ankle on the edge of the desk. "Spit it out already and let's get back to work."

"For one, *you* don't decide on Vi's baby shower. For heaven's sake, you stick your nose into everything."

"Excuse me?"

"But my main point is," she said, setting both hands at her hips, "I'm tired of being taken for granted."

"Who does that?" he asked, sincerely confused.

"*You* do!"

"Now, that's just not so," he argued. "Let's remember that raise yesterday and—"

"In the last day or so, you had me arrange for the new horse trailer to be dropped off at the ranch. I called Big Mike at the garage to get him to give your car a tune-up before the weekend, then I saw to it that the new horses you bought will be delivered to the ranch tomorrow afternoon."

Scowling now, Mac bit back on what he wanted to say and simply let her get it all out.

"I drew up the plans for the kitchen garden your cook wants for behind the house and I made sure the new baby furniture you're giving Vi was delivered on time." Andi paused only long enough to take a breath. Her eyes flashed, her mouth tightened as she continued. "Then I called Sheriff Battle to make sure he cleared the road for the delivery of the last of the cattle water tanks."

"Had to clear the road—"

"Not finished," she said, holding up one hand to keep him quiet. "After that, I bought and had delivered the standard half-carat diamond bracelet and the it's-not-you-it's-me farewell note to the model who can't string ten words together without hyperventilating…"

Mac snorted. All right, she had a point about Jezebel Fontaine. Still, in his defense, Jez was seriously built enough that he'd overlooked her lack of brain cells for the past month. But even he had his limits.

"You're my assistant, aren't you?"

"I am and a darn good one," she countered. "I've kept your life running on schedule for the last six years, Mac. No matter what you throw at me, I handle it and add it into the mix I'm already juggling."

"You're a damn fine juggler, too," he said.

She kept talking as if he hadn't said a thing.

"Then when I asked you for this afternoon off so I could go see my nephew's baseball game, you said you had to *think* about it. *Think about it?*"

"I appreciate a good Little League game as much as the next man," Mac said slowly, keeping his gaze fixed on hers, "but we've still got some details to be ironed out on the Double D deal and—"

"That's my point, Mac." His eyes widened when she interrupted him. "There's always *something* that needs to be handled and I'm so busy taking care of those things I haven't had time to find a *life*."

"You've got a pretty good life from where I'm standing," he argued, pushing up from his desk. "Great job, terrific boss—" He paused, waiting for a smile that didn't come, then tried to continue, but he couldn't come up with a third thing.

"Uh-huh. Job. Boss. No life." She took a deep breath. "And that stops today."

"Okay," he said flatly. "If it's that important to you, go. See your nephew's game. Have some popcorn. Hell, have a beer. We'll talk more tomorrow morning when you come in."

"I won't be in," she said, shaking her head. "It's time for a change, Mac. For both of us. I've gotten too comfortable here and so have you."

He laughed abruptly. "You call dealing with what all that's been going on around here *comfortable*?"

She nodded. "There've been problems, sure, but we handled them and things are slowly getting back to normal. Or, as normal as life gets around here."

Mac sure as hell hoped so. It had been a wild time in Royal, Texas, over the past couple of years. A lot of turmoil, more than their share of trouble. There was the tornado, of course, then the drought that held most of Texas in a tight, sweaty fist and then a man he used to think of as one of his oldest friends, Rafiq "Rafe" bin Saleed, had come to town with the express purpose of ruining Mac's reputation, his business and his family. And he'd come damn close to pulling it off.

Remembering that was still enough to leave Mac a little shaken. Hell, he'd trusted Rafe and had almost lost everything because of it. Sure, they'd worked everything out, and now Rafe was even his brother-in-law, since he and Mac's sister, Violet, were married and having a baby.

But there were still moments when Mac wondered how he could have missed the fact that Rafe was on a misguided quest for revenge.

Without Andi to help him through and talk him down when he was so damned angry he could hardly see straight, Mac didn't know if the situation would have resolved itself so quickly.

So why, when life was settling down again, had she chosen *now* to talk about quitting? Mac had no idea what had brought this nonsense on, but he'd nip it in the bud, fast. Now that things were calming down in Royal, Mac had plans to spend more time actually working and even expanding the family ranch, which Violet used to handle. With his sister focusing on the place Rafe had bought for them, Mac wanted to get back to his roots: being on a horse, overseeing the day-to-day decisions of ranch life and working out of a home office to keep his wildly divergent business interests growing.

Life was damn busy and Andi was just going to have to stay right where she was to help him run things—the way she always had.

"Where's this coming from, Andi?" he asked, leaning one hip against the corner of his desk.

"The fact that you can even ask me that is astonishing," she replied.

He gave her a slow grin, the very same smile that worked to sway women across Texas into agreeing with anything he said. Of course, Andrea Beaumont had always been a tougher sell, but he'd use whatever weapons he had to hand. "Now, Andi," he said, "we've worked together too long for you to get snippy so easily."

"Snippy?" Her eyes fired up again and Mac thought for a second or two that she might reach up and yank at her hair. "That is the most insulting thing…"

She took another deep breath and Mac idly noticed how those heavy breaths she kept taking made her small, perfect breasts rise and fall rhythmically. For such a tiny woman, she had curves in all the right places. Funny he'd really not taken the time to notice that before.

Andi was simply *there.* She kept on top of everything. Nothing ever slipped past her. But apparently *this* had slipped past *him.*

"This is coming out of the blue and I think you owe me some sort of explanation."

"It's *not* out of the blue, Mac," she said, throwing both hands high. "That's the point. I've worked for you for six years."

"I know that."

"Uh-huh. And did you notice I didn't even take a vacation the last two years?"

His frown deepened. No, he hadn't noticed. Probably should have, though, since every damn time she *did* take some time off, he ended up hunting her down, getting her to solve some damn problem or other. The fact that she'd stayed here, working, had only made his life continue on its smooth, well-planned path, so he hadn't had to think about it.

"Is that what this is about?" He pushed off the desk, braced his feet wide apart and folded his arms across his chest. "You want a vacation?"

Her mouth flattened into a straight, grim line. "No. I want a life. To get that life, I have to quit. So, I'm giving you my two weeks' notice."

"I don't accept that."

"You don't get a vote, Mac."

"See," he said tightly, "that doesn't fly with me, either."

It was like talking to two brick walls, Andrea thought, staring up at the man who had been her focus for the past six years. About six foot one, he had short, dark blond hair that in another month or so would be shot through with sun streaks. His summer-green eyes were cool, clear and always held a sort of calculating gleam his competitors usually took for affability. He was lean but strong, his build almost deceptively lanky.

Mac McCallum was the stuff women's dreams were made of. Sadly, that was true of Andi's dreams, too.

Six years she'd worked for him. She wasn't sure exactly when she'd made the supreme mistake of falling in love with her boss, but it seemed as if those feelings had always been with her. A part of her had always hoped that one day he might open his eyes and really *see* her—but the more rational, reasonable part of Andi knew that was never going to happen.

To Mac, she would always be good ol' Andi. She knew he saw her as he did the new laser printer in the office. Efficient, able to get the job done and nearly invisible. The raise he'd given her notwithstanding, he didn't really appreciate just how hard she worked to keep McCallum Enterprises running smoothly—he just expected it. Well, it had taken her a long time to reach this point, but she really wanted a life. And as long as she was here, mooning after a man she couldn't have, that wouldn't happen. Andi had been working up to quitting for a long while now, and today had finally given her the last little nudge she'd needed.

It was liberation day.

"Go on, Andi. Go to your nephew's game. Enjoy the rest of the day and we'll talk about this again when you calm down."

He still didn't get it, and she knew that she had to make herself clear. "I'm completely calm, Mac. I'm just done."

A slow, disbelieving smile curved his mouth, and Andi told herself to stay strong. Stay resolved. There was no future for her here. But watching him, she realized that he would spend her two weeks'-notice time doing everything he could to change her mind. Knowing just how charming he could be was enough to convince her to say, "I haven't had a vacation in two years. So I'm going to take my vacation time for the next two weeks."

"You're just going to leave the office flat?" Stunned now, he stared at her as if she had two heads. "What about the contracts for the Stevenson deal? Or the negotiations on the Franklin Heating project?"

"Laura's up-to-date on all of it and if she needs me," Andi said firmly, "she can call and I'll be happy to walk her through whatever problem she's having."

"Laura's the office manager."

True, Andi thought, and though the woman had been with the company for only a couple of years, she was bright, ambitious and a hard worker. And as a newly-wed, she wouldn't be spinning romantic fantasies about her boss.

"You're serious?" he asked, dumbfounded. *"Now?"*

"Right now," Andi told him and felt a faint flutter of excitement tangled with just a touch of fear.

She was really going to do it. Going to quit the job she'd dedicated herself to for years. Going to walk away from the man who had a hold on her heart whether he knew it or not. She was going out into the world to find herself a life.

With that thought firmly in mind, she turned and headed for the door before Mac could talk her out of leaving.

"I don't believe this," he muttered.

Can't really blame him, she thought. This was the first time since she'd met Mac that she was doing something for herself.

Andi paused in the doorway and glanced back over her shoulder for one last look at him. He was everything she'd ever wanted and she'd finally accepted that she would never have him. "Goodbye, Mac."

Outside, the June sunlight streamed down from a brassy blue sky. Summer was coming and it seemed in a hurry to get here. Andi's footsteps crunched on the gravel of the employee parking area behind the office.

With every step, she felt a little more certain that what she was doing was right. Sure, it was hard, and likely to get harder because Andi would miss seeing Mac every day. But hadn't she spent enough time mooning over him? How would she ever find a man to spend her life with if she spent all her time around the one man she couldn't have?

"Just keep walking, Andi. You'll be glad of it later." Much later, of course. Because at the moment, she felt as if she couldn't breathe.

What she needed was affirmation and she knew just where to find it. When she got to her car, Andi opened the door and slid into the dark blue compact. Then she pulled her cell phone from her purse, hit the speed dial and waited through five rings before a familiar voice answered.

"Thank God you called," her sister, Jolene, said. "Tom's shift ended two hours ago and now that he's home, he says he needs to unwind…"

Andi laughed and it felt good. "So which wall is he tearing down?"

Jolene sighed. "The one between the living room and the kitchen."

While her sister talked, Andi could picture exactly what was happening in the old Victorian on the far side of Royal. Her brother-in-law, Tom, was a fireman who relaxed by working on his house. Last year, after a brush-fire that had kept him working for more than a week, he built a new powder room on the first floor.

"It's a good thing you bought a fixer-upper," Andi said when her older sister had wound down.

"I know." Laughing, Jolene added, "I swear the man's crazy. But he's all mine."

Andi smiled sadly, caught her expression in the rear-view mirror and silently chastised herself for feeling even the slightest twinge of envy. Jolene and Tom had been married for ten years and had three kids, with another on the way. Their family was a sort of talisman for Andi. Seeing her sister happy and settled with her family made Andi want the same for herself.

Which was just one of the reasons she'd had to quit her job. Before it was too late for her to find what her heart craved. Love. Family.

"And," Jolene was saying, "I love that my kitchen's about to get a lot bigger. But oh, Lord, the noise. Hang on, I'm headed out to the front porch so I can hear you."

Andi listened to the crashing and banging in the background fade as her sister walked farther away from the demolition zone.

"Okay, backyard. That's better," Jolene said. "So, what's going on, little sister?"

"I did it." Andi blew out a breath and rolled her car windows down to let the warm Texas wind slide past her. "I quit."

"Holy…" Jolene paused and Andi imagined her sister's shocked expression. "Really? You quit your job?"

"I did." Andi slapped one hand to her chest to keep her pounding heart from leaping out. "Walked right out before I could change my mind."

"I can't believe it."

"You and me both," Andi said. "Oh, God. I'm *unemployed*."

Jolene laughed. "It's not like you're living on the streets, Andi. You've got a house you hardly ever see, a vacation fund that you've never used and a rainy-day savings account that has enough in it to keep you safe through the next biblical flood."

"You're right, you're right." Nodding, Andi took a few deep breaths and told herself to calm down. "It's just, I haven't been unemployed since I was sixteen."

The reality of the situation was hitting home and it came like a fist to the solar plexus. If this kept up, she might faint and wouldn't that be embarrassing, having Mac come out to the parking lot and find her stretched out across her car seats?

She'd quit her job.

What would she do every day? How would she live? Sure, she'd had a few ideas over the past few months about what she might want to do, but none of it was carved in stone. She hadn't looked into the logistics of anything, she hadn't made even the first list of what she'd need do before moving on one of her ideas, so it was all too nebulous to even think about.

She had time. Plenty of time to consider her future, to look at her ideas objectively. She would need plans. Purpose. Goals. But she wasn't going to have those right away, so it was time to take a breath. No point in making herself totally insane. Jolene was right. Andi had a big savings account—Mac was a generous employer if nothing else—and it wasn't as if she'd had time to spend that generous salary. Now she did.

"This is so great, Andi."

"Easy for you to say."

Jolene laughed again, then shouted, "Jilly, don't push your sister into the pool."

Anyone else hearing that would immediately think built-in, very deep pool. In reality, Andi knew the kids were jumping in and out of a two-foot-deep wading pool. Shallow enough to be safe and wet enough to give relief from the early Texas heat.

"Jacob's game still at five today?" Andi asked abruptly.

"Sure. You're coming?"

Of course she was going to the game. She'd quit her job so she'd be able to see her family. She smiled at her reflection as she imagined the look on Jacob's little face when she showed up at the town baseball field. "You couldn't keep me away."

"Look at that—only been unemployed like a second and already you're getting a life."

Andi rolled her eyes. Jolene had been on her to quit for the past few years, insisting that standing still meant stagnating. As it turned out, she had a point. Andi had given Mac all she could give. If she stayed, she'd only end up resenting him and infuriated with herself. So it was no doubt past time to go. Move on.

And on her first official day of freedom, she was going to the Royal Little League field to watch her nephew's game. "I'm just going home to change and I'll meet you at the field in an hour or so."

"We'll be there. Jacob will be so excited. And after the game, you'll come back here. Tom will grill us all some steaks to go with the bottle of champagne I'm making a point of picking up. You can drink my share."

Andi forced a smile into her voice. "Champagne and steaks. Sounds like a plan."

But after she hung up with her sister, Andi had to ask herself why, instead of celebrating, she felt more like going home for a good cry.

Two

Andi went to the baseball game. Jolene had been right: eight-year-old Jacob was thrilled that his aunt was there, cheering for him alongside his parents. Of course, six-year-old Jilly and three-year-old Jenna were delighted to share their bag of gummy bears with Andi, and made plans for a tea party later in the week.

It had felt odd to be there, in the bleachers with family and friends, when normally she would have been at work. But it was good, too, she kept telling herself.

After the game, she had dinner with her family and every time her mind drifted to thoughts of Mac, Andi forced it away again. Instead, she focused on the kids, her sister and the booming laugh of her brother-in-law as he flipped steaks on a smoking grill.

By the following morning, she told herself that if she'd stayed with Mac and kept the job that had consumed her life, she wouldn't have had that lazy, easy afternoon and evening. But still she had doubts. Even though she'd enjoyed herself, the whole thing had been so far out of her comfort zone, Andi knew she'd have to do some fine-tuning of her relaxation skills. But at least now she had the time to try.

Sitting on her front porch swing, cradling a cup of coffee in her hands, Andi looked up at the early-morning sky and saw her own nebulous future staring back at her. Normally by this time she was already at the office, brewing the first of many pots of coffee, going over her and Mac's calendars and setting up conference calls and meetings. There would already be the kind of tension she used to live for as she worked to keep one step ahead of everything.

Now? She took another sip of coffee and sighed. The quiet crowded in on her until it felt as though she could hear her own heartbeat in the silence. Relaxation turned to tension in a finger snap. She was unemployed and, for the first time since she was a kid, had nowhere in particular to be.

It was both liberating and a little terrifying. She was a woman who thrived on schedules, preferred order and generally needed a plan for anything she was going to do. Even as a kid, she'd had her closet tidy, her homework done early and her bookcases in her room alphabetized for easy reference.

While Jolene's bedroom had been chaotic, Andi's was an island of peace and calm. A place for everything, everything in its place. Some might call that compulsive. She called it organized. And maybe that was just what she needed to do now. Organize her new world. Channel energies she would normally be using for Mac and his business into her own life. She was smart, capable and tenacious. There was nothing she couldn't do.

"So." After that inner pep talk, she drew her feet up under her on the thick, deep blue cushion. "I'll make a plan. Starting," she said, needing the sound of her own voice in the otherwise still air, "with finally getting my house in shape."

She'd bought the run-down farmhouse a year ago and hadn't even had the time to unpack most of the boxes stacked in the second bedroom. The walls hadn't been painted, there were no pictures hung, no rugs scattered across the worn, scarred floor. It pretty much looked as lonely and abandoned as it had when she first bought it. And wasn't that all kinds of sad and depressing?

Until a year ago, Andi had lived in a tiny condo that was, in its own way, as impersonal and unfinished as this house. She'd rented it furnished and had never had the time—or the inclination—to put her own stamp on the place. Working for Mac had meant that she was on duty practically twenty-four hours a day. So when was she supposed to be able to carve out time for herself? But in spite of everything, Andi had wanted a home of her own. And in the back of her mind, maybe she'd been planning even then on leaving McCallum Enterprises.

Leaving Mac.

It was the only explanation for her buying a house that she had known going in would need a lot of renovation. Sure, she could have hired a crew to come in and fix it all up. And she had had a new roof put on, the plumbing upgraded and the electrical brought up to code. But there were still the yards to take care of, the floors to be sanded, the walls to be painted and furniture to be bought.

"And that starts today," she said, pushing off the swing. With one more look around the wide front yard, she turned and opened the screen door, smiling as it screeched in protest. Inside, she took another long glance at her home before heading into the kitchen to do what she did best. Make a list.

She knew where she'd start. The walls should be painted before she brought in sanders for the floors, and they'd probably need a couple of coats of paint to cover the shadow images of long-missing paintings.

In the kitchen she sat at a tiny table and started making notes. She'd go at her home exactly as she would have a new project at McCallum. Priorities. It was all about priorities.

An hour later, she had several lists and the beginnings of a plan.

"There's a lot to do," she said, her voice echoing in the old, empty house. "Might as well get started."

She worked for hours, sweeping, dusting, mopping, before heading into Royal to buy several gallons of paint. Of course, shopping in town was never as easy as entering a store, getting what you wanted and then leaving again. There were people to chat with, gossip to listen to and, as long as she was there, she stopped in at the diner for some tea and a salad she didn't have to make herself.

The air conditioning felt wonderful against her skin, and Andi knew if it was this hot in early June, summer was going to be a misery. She made a mental note to put in a call to Joe Bennet at Bennet Heating and Cooling. If she was going to survive a Texas summer, she was going to need her own air conditioning. Fast.

"So," Amanda Battle said as she gave Andi a refill on

her iced tea. "I hear you quit your job and you're running off to Jamaica with your secret lover."

Andi choked on a cherry tomato and, when she got her breath back, reached for her tea and took a long drink. Looking up at Amanda, wife of Sheriff Nathan Battle and owner of the diner, she saw humor shining in her friend's eyes.

"Jamaica?"

Amanda grinned. "Sally Hartsfield told me, swears that Margie Fontenot got the story direct from Laura, who used to work with you at Mac's. Well, Laura's cousin's husband's sister got the story started and that is good enough to keep the grapevine humming for a while."

Direct was probably not the right word to describe that line of communication, but Andi knew all too well how the gossip chain worked in town. It was only mildly irritating to find out that she was now the most interesting link in that chain. For the moment.

But Jamaica? How did people come up with this stuff? she wondered, and only briefly considered taking her first vacation in years, if only to make that rumor true. Still, if she went to Jamaica, it would be a lot more fun if she could make the secret-lover part of the gossip true, too.

"Secret lover?" If only, she thought wistfully as an image of Mac rose up in her mind.

"Oooh. I like how your eyes got all shiny there for a second. Tells me there might be something to this particular rumor. Something you'd like to share with a pal? Wait." Amanda held up one finger. "Gotta fill some coffee cups. Don't go anywhere until I get back."

While she was gone, Andi concentrated on the sounds and scents of the Royal Diner. Everything was so familiar; sitting there was like being wrapped up in a cozy blanket. Even when you knew that everyone in town was now talking about *you*. Royal had had plenty of things to chew over the past couple years. From the tornado to an actual *sheikh* working a revenge plot against Mac, local tongues had been kept wagging.

And the diner was gossip central—well, here and the Texas Cattleman's Club. But since the club was limited to members only, Andi figured the diner was the big winner in the grapevine contest.

She looked around and pretended not to notice when other customers quickly shifted their gazes. The black-and-white-tile floor was spotless, the red vinyl booths and counter stools were shiny and clean, and the place, as always, was packed.

God, she hated knowing that mostly everyone in there was now talking and speculating about her. But short of burying her head in the sand or locking herself in her own house, there was no way to avoid any of it.

Amanda worked the counter while her sister, Pamela, and Ruby Fowler worked the tables. Conversations rose and fell like the tides, and the accompanying sounds of silverware against plates and the clink of glasses added a sort of background music to the pulse of life.

When Amanda finally came back, Andi mused, "Where did Laura come up with Jamaica, I wonder?"

"Nothing on the secret lover then?" Amanda asked.

Andi snorted. "Who has time for a lover?"

Amanda gave her a sympathetic look, reached out and patted her hand. "Honey, that's so sad. You've got to make time."

She would if she had the option of the lover she wanted. But since she didn't, why bother with anyone else? "How can I when I'm going to Jamaica? But again, why Jamaica?"

"Maybe wishful thinking," Amanda said with a shrug, leaning down to brace folded arms on the counter. "Heaven knows, lying on a beach having somebody bring me lovely alcoholic drinks while I cuddle with my honey sounds pretty good to me most days."

"Okay, sounds pretty good to me, too," Andi said. If she *had* a honey. "Instead, I'm headed home to start painting."

Amanda straightened up. "You're planning on painting your place on your own? It'll take you weeks."

"As the gossip chain informed you already," she said wryly, "I'm unemployed, so I've got some time."

"Well," Amanda said, walking to the register to ring up Andi's bill, "using that time to paint rather than find yourself that secret lover seems a waste to me. And, if you change your mind, there's any number of kids around town who would paint for you. Summer jobs are hard to come by in a small town."

"I'll keep it in mind. Thanks." Andi paid, slung her purse over her shoulder and said, "Say hi to Nathan for me."

"I'll do that. And say hi to Jamaica for me." Amanda gave her a wink, then went off to check on her customers again.

Several hours later, Andi knew she should have been tired. Instead, she was energized, and by the end of her first day as a free woman, the living room was painted a cool, rich green the color of the Texas hills in springtime. It would need another coat, but even now she saw the potential and loved it. She had a sense of accomplishment, of simple satisfaction, which she hadn't felt in far too long. Yes, she'd been successful in her career, but that was Mac's business. His empire. This little farmhouse, abandoned for years, was all *hers*. And she was going to bring it back to life. Make it shine as it had to some long-gone family.

"And maybe by the time it's whole and happy again, I will be, too," she said.

"Talking to yourself?" a female voice said from the front porch. "Not a good sign."

Andi spun around and grinned. "Violet! Come on in."

Mac's sister opened the screen door and let it slap closed behind her. Being nearly seven months pregnant hadn't stopped Vi from dressing like the rancher she was. She wore a pale yellow T-shirt that clung to her rounded belly, a pair of faded blue jeans and the dusty brown boots she preferred to anything else.

Her auburn hair was pulled into a high ponytail at the back of her head and her clear green eyes swept the freshly painted walls in approval. When she looked back at Andi, she nodded. "Nice job. Really. Love the darker green as trim, too. Makes the whole thing pop."

"Thanks." Andi took another long look and sighed. "I'll go over it again tomorrow. But I love it. This color makes the room feel cool, you know? And with summer coming…"

"It's already hot," Vi said. "You are getting air conditioning put in, right?"

"Oh, yeah. Called them at about eight this morning, as soon as the sun came up and started sizzling. They're backed up, though, so it'll be a week or two before they can come out here."

"Well," Vi said, walking into the kitchen as comfortably as she would at her own house. "If you start melting before then, you can come and stay with Rafe and me at the ranch."

"Ah, yes," Andi said, following her friend into her kitchen—which was comfortably stuck in the 1950s. "What a good time. I can be the third wheel with the newlyweds."

"We don't have sex in front of people, you know," Vi told her with a laugh. "We tried, but the housekeeper Rafe hired disapproved."

She stuck her head in the refrigerator, pulled out a pitcher of tea and sighed with pleasure. "Knew I could count on you to have tea all ready to go. You get glasses. Do you have any cookies?"

"Some Oreos." They'd been friends for so long, they worked in tandem. "In the pantry."

"Thank God."

Laughing, Andi filled two glasses with ice, then poured each of them some tea as Vi hurried into the walk-in pantry and came back out already eating a cookie. She sighed, rolled her eyes and moaned, "God, these are so good."

Still chuckling, Andi took a seat at the tiny table and watched her friend dig into the cookie bag for another. "Rafe still watching what you eat?"

Vi dropped into the chair opposite her, picked up her tea and took a long drink. "Like a hawk. He found my stash of Hershey's bars, so they're gone." She ate the next cookie with as much relish as she had the first. "I love the man like crazy but he's making me a little nuts. Although, one thing I'll say for him, he does keep ice cream stocked for me."

"Well, that's something," Andi agreed, taking a seat opposite her.

"But, wow, I miss cookies. And cake. And brownies. The only bad part about moving to the Wild Aces when I married Rafe? Leaving the Double M and our housekeeper Teresa's brownies. I swear they're magic." Vi sighed and reached for another cookie. "You want to make a batch of brownies?"

Andi really hated to quash the hopeful look on her friend's face, but said, "Oven doesn't work." Andi turned to look at the pastel pink gas stove. The burners worked fine, but the oven had been dead for years, she was willing to bet. "And it's too hot in here to bake anything."

"True." Vi turned her tea glass on the narrow kitchen table, studying the water ring it left behind. "And I didn't really come here to raid your pantry, either, in spite of the fact that I'm eating all of your Oreos."

"Okay, then why are you here?"

"I'm a spy," Violet said, laughing. "And I'm here to report that Mac is really twisted up about you quitting."

"Is he?" Well, that felt good, didn't it? She had long known that she was indispensable in the office. Now he knew it, too, and that thought brought her an immense wave of satisfaction. Instantly, a ping of guilt began to echo inside her, but Andi shut it down quickly. After all, it wasn't as if she *wanted* Mac to have a hard time. She was only taking the opportunity to enjoy the fact that he was. "How do you know?"

"Well, spy work isn't easy," Violet admitted. "We pregnant operatives must rely on information from reliable sources."

Andi laughed shortly. "You mean gossip."

"I resent that term," Violet said with an indignant

sniff. Then she shrugged and took another cookie. "Although, it's accurate. Mac hasn't actually said anything to me directly. *Yet.* But Laura called a couple hours ago practically in tears."

"What happened?" Andi asked. "Mac's not the kind of man to bring a woman to tears."

"I don't know," Violet said, smiling. "He's made me cry a few times."

"Angry tears don't count."

"Then Laura's tears don't count, either," Vi told her. "She was really mad—at *you* for leaving her alone in the office."

"Probably why she made up the Jamaica story," Andi muttered.

"Jamaica?"

"Never mind." She waved one hand to brush that away. "What did Mac do?"

"Nothing new. Just the same old crabby attitude you've been dealing with for years. Laura just doesn't know how to deal with it yet."

Okay, now she felt a little guilty. Mac could be…difficult. And maybe she should have used her two weeks' notice to prepare Laura for handling him. But damn it, *she'd* learned on her own, hadn't she? Laura was just going to have to suck it up and deal.

"Anyway," Vi continued, "I told her the best thing to do was stay out of his way when he starts grumbling under his breath. She said that's exactly what he was doing already and that the office was too small for her to effectively disappear."

Andi chuckled because she could imagine the woman trying to hunch into invisibility behind her desk. "Poor Laura. I really shouldn't laugh, though, should I? I sort of left her holding the bag, so to speak, and now she's having to put up with not only Mac's demands but the fact that I'm not there to take the heat off."

"Laura's tough. She can take it." Vi picked up a fourth cookie and sighed a little as she bit in. "Or she won't. Either way, her choice. And if she walks out, too? An even better lesson for Mac."

"You think?"

"Absolutely," his sister said, waving her cookie for emphasis before popping it into her mouth and talking around it while she chewed. "The man thinks he's the center of the universe and all the rest of us are just moons orbiting him.

"Maybe it really started when our parents died and he had to step up. You know, he's only six years older than me, but he went from big brother to overbearing father figure in a finger snap." She frowned a little, remembering. "We butted heads a lot, but in the end, Mac always found a way to win."

Andi knew most of this family history. Over the years, Mac had talked to her about the private plane crash that had claimed his parents and how he'd worked to make sure that Violet felt safe and secure despite the tragedy that had rocked their family. He'd done it, too. Violet was not only a successful, happy adult, she was married and about to become a mother.

Maybe he had been overbearing—and knowing Mac, she really had no doubt of that—but he'd protected his sister, kept the family ranch and even managed to build on the business his parents had left behind until McCallum Enterprises was one of the biggest, most diversified companies in the country.

In all fairness to him, Andi had to say, "Looks to me like he did a good job."

Violet shrugged and nodded. "Yeah, he did. But the thing is, he's so used to people snapping to attention whenever he walks into a room, I think it's good for him that you quit. That he's finding out he can't *always* win. It'll be a growth moment for him."

But Andi knew that growth wasn't always easy. She also knew she should feel bad about being glad that Mac would have a hard time without her.

Apparently, though, she wasn't that good a person.

She still wasn't there.

From the moment Mac walked into the office that morning, a part of him had fully expected to find Andi right where she belonged, at her desk. But she hadn't been.

Except for a few times when he'd had no other choice, Mac had spent most of the day ignoring Laura as she hunched behind her computer, pretending to be invisible. No doubt she'd been worried how the day would go without Andi there to take care of things.

Well, hell, he had been, too.

As it turned out, with reason.

"This day just couldn't get worse."

Mac left his office and fired a hard look at Laura. "I need the Franklin contracts. I tried to pull up the pdf and it's not where it's supposed to be. Bob Franklin just called, he's got some questions and—" He noticed the wide-eyed expression on Laura's face and told himself it was pointless to hammer at her.

This was Andi's territory. Turning, he stomped into the back of the building where Andi had stored hard copies of each of their in-progress deals in old-fashioned file cabinets. Of course, their records were mostly digitized and stored in the cloud, with several redundant backup sites so nothing could be lost. But there was something to say for holding a hard copy of a contract in your hands. It was immediate and more convenient, in his mind, than scrolling up and down a computer screen looking for a particular clause. Especially when you couldn't find the damn digital copy.

"And now I have to hunt down the stupid contract the hard way." He yanked open the top file drawer and started flipping through the manila separators. He made it through the *F*s and didn't find the Franklin takeover.

Shaking his head, he told himself that he was the damn *boss*. It wasn't up to him to find a damn contract on a damn deal they'd done only three weeks ago. The problem was it was *Andi's* job and she wasn't here to do it.

Laura was good at what she did and he had no doubt that in time she might grow to be even a third as good as Andi at the job. But for now, the woman was an office manager suddenly tossed into the deep end. There were a couple of part-time interns, too, but neither of them could find their way out of a paper bag without a flashlight and a map.

"So bottom line?" he muttered, slamming the drawer and then opening another one. "I'm screwed."

Normally, this late in the afternoon, he and Andi were huddled around his desk, talking about the day's work and what was coming up on the schedule. He really didn't want to admit how much he missed just talking to her. Having her there to bounce ideas off of. To help him strategize upcoming jobs.

"Plus, she would know exactly where the stupid contract is," he muttered.

Mac hated this. Hated having his life disrupted, his business interfered with—hell, his *world* set off balance. Worse, Andi had to have known this would happen when she walked out and, no doubt, she was sitting on a beach in Bimini right now, smiling at the thought of him trying to set things right again on his own.

"Take a vacation. Who the hell has time for a vacation?" he asked the empty file room. "If you love what you do, *work* is vacation enough, isn't it?" He slammed the second drawer shut and yanked the third open. What the hell kind of filing system was she using, anyway?

"She loved her work, too," he muttered. "Can't tell me otherwise. In charge of every damn thing here, wasn't she? Even setting up the damn filing system in some weird way that I can't figure out now. If she thinks I'm going to let this damn office crumble to the ground then she's got another damn think or two coming to her because damned if I will, damn it!"

Temper spiking, he slammed the third drawer shut and then just stood there, hands on his hips, and did a slow turn, taking in the eight filing cabinets and the dust-free work table and chairs in the center of the room.

"Why the hell is she on a beach when I need her help?"

His brain dredged up a dreamlike image of Andi, lying back on some lounge, beneath a wide umbrella. She sipped at a frothy drink and behind huge sunglasses, her eyes smiled. Some cabana boy hovered nearby enjoying the view of Andi in a tiny yellow bikini that Mac's mind assured him was filled out perfectly.

Mac scowled and shut down that mental image because he sure as hell didn't need it. "Why is she off enjoying herself when I'm here trying to figure out what she did?"

But even as he complained, he knew it wasn't the filing that bothered him. Given enough time, he'd find whatever he needed to find. It was being here. In the office. Without Andi.

All day he'd felt slightly off balance. One step out of rhythm. It had started when he got there early as usual and didn't smell coffee. Andi had always beat him to work and had the coffee going for both of them. Then she'd carry two cups into his office and they'd go over the day's schedule and the plans that were constantly in motion.

Not today, though. He'd made his own damn coffee—he wasn't a moron after all—then had carried it to his desk and sat there alone, going over schedules that *she* had set up. She wasn't there to talk to. She wasn't there to remind him to keep on track and not to go spinning off into tangents—so his brain had taken one of those side roads and he'd lost two hours of time while researching an idea on the internet. So the rest of the day he was behind schedule and that was her fault, too.

"What the hell is she doing in Bimini? Or Tahiti or wherever it is she went looking to relax?" Shaking his head, he walked to the window and stared out as the twilight sky deepened into lavender and the first stars winked into existence.

In the distance, he could see the fields of his home ranch, the Double M, freshly planted and only waiting for summer heat to grow and thrive and become a sea of waving, deep, rich green alfalfa. Beyond those fields lay miles of open prairie, where his cattle wandered freely and the horses he wanted to focus on raising and breeding raced across open ground, tails and manes flying.

This was his place. His home. His empire.

He'd taken over from his father when his parents died and Mac liked to think they'd have been proud of what he'd done with their legacy. He'd improved it, built on it and had plans that would continue to make it grow and thrive.

"And it would be a helluva lot easier to do if Andi hadn't chucked it all for the beach and a margarita."

When his phone rang, he reached for it, digging it out of his pocket. Seeing his sister's name pop up didn't put a smile on his face. "What is it, Vi?"

"Well, hello to you, too," she said, laughing in his ear. "Nothing like family to give you that warm, fuzzy feeling."

He sighed, scraped one hand across his face and searched for patience. He and Vi had been at odds most of their lives, especially since he had been in charge of her and Vi didn't take kindly to anyone giving her orders. Through it all, though, they'd remained close, which he was grateful for.

Usually.

Already annoyed, he didn't need much of a push to pass right into irritated. "What is it, Vi? I'm busy."

"Wow, I'm just choking up with all this sentiment. Must be all these hormones from being pregnant with your first niece or nephew."

Reluctantly, Mac smiled. Shaking his head, he leaned back against the nearest cabinet and said, "Point made. Okay then, what's going on, little sister?"

"Oh, nothing much. Just wanted to see how you were

holding up—you know," she added in a sly tone, "with Andi gone and all."

"Heard about that, did you?" Hadn't taken long, Mac thought. But then the only thing that moved faster than a Texas tornado was gossip in Royal. He hated knowing that the whole town was talking about him.

Again. During that mess with Rafe, the McCallum family had been pretty much front and center on everyone's radar. With that settled, he'd expected life to go back to normal. Which it would have if Andi hadn't gotten a wild hair up her—

"Of course I heard," Vi was saying, and he could tell by her voice she was enjoying herself. "People all over town are talking about it and I figured Laura could use some advice on how to defuse your temper."

"Temper?" He scowled and shifted his gaze back to the view out the window. He realized it was later than he thought, as he watched Laura hurrying across the parking lot to her car. He sighed when she glanced back at the building uneasily. Hell, he'd be lucky if Laura didn't desert him, too. Still, he felt as though he had to defend himself. "I don't have a temper—"

Violet laughed and the sound rolled on and on until she was nearly gasping for breath. "Oh my, Mac. That was a good one."

He scowled a little as Laura drove out of the lot, then he shifted his gaze to the twilight just creeping across the sky. "Glad you're having a fine time."

"Well, come on," she said, laughter still evident in her tone. "Don't you remember the roof-raising shouting you used to do at me when I was a kid?"

"Shouting's not temper," he argued, "that's communication."

"Okay, sure," she said, chuckling. "Anyway, how's it going in the office without Andi there riding herd on everything?"

"It's *my* business, Vi," he reminded her. "I think I can take care of it on my own."

"That bad, huh?"

His back teeth ground together and he took a tight grip on the shout that wanted to erupt from his throat. It would only prove his sister right about his temper. And yeah, she was right about Andi being gone, too. It wasn't easy. Harder, frankly, than he'd thought it would be. But he wouldn't admit it. Wouldn't say so to Vi and for damn sure wouldn't be calling Andi to ask for help while she sat on some beach sipping cocktails. She'd made her choice, he told himself. Walked away from her responsibilities—from *him*—without a backward glance.

"Well, when I saw Andi earlier, she was doing just fine, in case you were interested..."

He came to attention. "You *saw* her? Where?"

"Her house."

Mac frowned out the window at the darkening sky. "She said she was taking her vacation time."

"And she's using it to fix up the house she's barely seen since she bought it."

He heard the dig in there and he wouldn't apologize for working so much. And as his assistant, Andi had been expected to spend as much time as he did at the job—and she'd never complained until now.

"With what I pay her as my executive assistant," he argued, "Andi could have hired crews of men to pull that house together at any point in the last year."

"Speaking of points," his sister said, "you're missing

Andi's entirely. She wants a *life*, Mac. Something you should think about, too."

"My life is just fine."

"Right. It's why you're living in the big ranch house all by yourself and the last date you had was with that airhead model who had trouble spelling her own name."

Mac snorted. She had a point about Jez. But when a man dated a woman like that, he wasn't worrying about her IQ.

"You realize you're supposed to be on *my* side in this?"

"Strangely enough, I am on your side, Mac. You're the most hardheaded man I've ever known—and that includes my darling husband, Rafe."

"Thanks very much," he muttered.

"I'm just saying," Vi went on, "maybe you could learn something from Andi on this."

"You want me to quit, too? You ready to take over?"

She laughed and he could almost see her rolling her eyes. "A vacation isn't the end of the world, Mac. Even for you."

While Vi talked, telling him all about the new nursery she and Rafe were having designed, Mac's mind once again focused on Andi.

Why in hell she'd all of a sudden gone off the rails, he still didn't understand. But if she was here in Texas and not being waited on by hot-and-cold-running cabana boys, maybe he could find out.

He smiled to himself. And maybe, he could convince her that quitting this job was the biggest mistake she'd ever made.

Three

It had been a long day, but a good one.

Andi was feeling pretty smug about her decision to quit and was deliberately ignoring the occasional twinges of regret. She'd done the right thing, leaving her job and—though it pained her—Mac behind. In fact, she should have done it three years ago. As soon as she realized that she was in love with a man who would never see her as more than a piece of office equipment.

Her heart ached a little, but she took another sip of wine and deliberately drowned that pain. Once she was free of her idle daydreams of Mac, she'd be able to look around, find a man to be with. To help her build the life she wanted so badly. A house. Children. A job that didn't eat up every moment of her time until it was all she could do to squeeze out a few minutes for a shower every day.

Shaking her head clear of any thoughts at all, she

sipped her wine and focused on the TV. The old movie playing was one of her favorites. And *The Money Pit* seemed particularly apt at this moment. The house needed a lot of work, but now she had the time and the money to put into it. It occurred to her that she was actually nesting and she liked it. The smell of fresh paint wafted through the room, even with the windows open to catch whatever the early-summer breeze might stir up. It was a warm night, but Andi was too tired to care. Her arms ached from wielding a roller all day, but it felt good. So good, in fact, she didn't even grumble when someone knocked on the front door, disturbing her relaxation period.

Wineglass in hand, she answered the door and jolted when she saw Mac smiling at her from across the threshold. He was absolutely the last person she would have expected to find on her porch.

"Mac? What're you doing here?"

"Hello to you, too," he said and stepped past her, unasked, into the house.

All she could do was close the door and follow him into the living room.

He turned a slow circle, taking in the room, and she looked at her house through his eyes. The living room had scarred wooden floors, a couch and coffee table and a small end table with a lamp, turned on now against the twilight gloom. The attached dining room was empty but for the old built-in china cabinet, and the open doorway into the kitchen showed off that room's flaws to perfection.

The whole house looked like a badly furnished rental, not like someone's home. But then, in her defense, she hadn't had the opportunity before now to really make a difference in the old house. Still, her newly painted soft green walls looked great.

He sniffed. "Been painting."

"Good guess."

He turned around, gave her a quick smile that had her stomach jittering before she could quash her automatic response. "I can smell it. The color's good."

"Thanks. Mac, why are you here?"

"First off," he said, "where the hell did you file the Franklin contracts?"

She hadn't been expecting that. "Alphabetically in the cabinet marked *T* for *takeovers*. There's also a *B* for *buyouts* and *M* for *mergers*."

He whipped his hat off and ran his fingers through his hair. "Of course there is."

"Laura could have told you this."

"Laura's not speaking to me."

"You scared her, didn't you," Andi said, shaking her head.

"I'm not scary."

"You don't scare *me*."

"Maybe I should," he muttered, then shrugged. "I'm also here because I wanted to get a look at what you left me for."

"You make it sound like I'm your cheating wife." She sighed. "I didn't leave you. I left my job."

But she *had* left him, Mac thought. It didn't feel like an employee walking out, but a betrayal. Damn it, she'd taught him over the years to count on her. To depend on her for too many things—and then she was gone. How the hell else was he supposed to feel?

"Same thing." His gaze fixed on her and for the first time he noticed that she wore a tiny tank top and a silky pair of drawstring pants. Her feet were bare and her toe-nails were painted a soft, blush pink. Her hair was long and loose over her shoulders, just skimming the tops of her breasts.

Mac took a breath and wondered where that flash of heat swamping him had come from. He'd been with Andi nearly every day for the past six years and he'd never reacted to her like this before. Sure, she was pretty, but she was his assistant. The one stable, organized, efficient woman in his life and he'd never taken the time to notice that she was so much more than that.

Now it was all he could notice.

Dragging his gaze from her, he took a deep breath and looked down the short hall toward the back of the house. "Do I get a tour?"

"No." She really wanted him out of there. He had to wonder why. "I painted all day. I'm tired. So—"

He looked back at her and thought she didn't look tired to him. She looked downright edible. "You don't have to do it all yourself, Andi. I could have a crew out here tomorrow and they'd be done with the whole place by the end of the week."

"I enjoy painting."

He shot her a speculative look. "You enjoy hacking your way through jungles, too? A team of gardeners could tear out those briars growing wild by the front porch."

"I don't want to hire someone—"

"I said I would hire them."

"No."

"Why the hell not?" He could understand stubbornness. Hell, he sort of admired it. But this was pure mule-headedness. There was no reason for her to work herself into the ground trying to prove a point. "People who own houses hire people to work on them all the time."

"You don't get it, Mac," she said. "I want to do the work."

"You obviously need the help." He gave another quick look around. He could see what his sister had meant. The house did seem to be practically void of any kind of personal decoration or warmth. "You've been here—what? A year? As organized as you are, it shouldn't have taken you nearly that long to whip this place into shape. But it looks like you've hardly touched it."

Insult shot through her tone. "Seriously? When was I supposed to do any of that? I spend—spent—all of my time at the office. And on those extremely rare—I'm talking bigfoot-sighting rare—occasions when I did get an entire weekend off, I tried to squeeze in a little family time. See people. Go outside."

Mac rubbed one hand across the back of his neck and wished he could argue with her, but he knew she was right. He had pretty much monopolized her every waking moment for the past six years. But it wasn't as if he'd held her hostage. She'd made a hell of a lot of money thanks to the job she'd walked away from so easily.

"You don't have to make it sound like you were in prison," he pointed out in his own defense. "You love the work as much as I do."

"I do enjoy the work, and I'm good at it," she added as if he needed reminding. "But I want more out of life than closeting myself up in an office."

"And painting your house yourself, digging out briars and a mountain of weeds like I've never seen before, is 'more'?"

She frowned and he felt her irritation coming at him in thick waves. "For now, yes."

"You really must be desperate if you call painting and gardening a vacation," he said, watching her. "I really expected the rumor about you and Jamaica was true and you were off having silly drinks in coconut shells."

That mental image of Andi in a bathing suit rose up in his mind again, and now, thanks to seeing her out of her normal buttoned-down attire, his imagination was doing a much better job of filling out that dream bikini.

She huffed out a breath, folded her arms over her middle, unconsciously lifting her breasts high enough that he got a peek at the tops of them thanks to the scoop-necked tank she wore. A buzz of electricity zapped Mac and he had to work to keep his own hormones in line. How had he spent six years with this woman and *not* noticed how nicely she was put together?

She'd always worn her long, straight brown hair pulled back in a businesslike knot or ponytail, so until tonight he never would have guessed that it was wavy when she let it down around her shoulders—or that lamplight brought out hidden golden streaks among the dark brown. Andi had always worn sensible, straitlaced clothing on the job, so seeing her in that sleeveless tank and loose, silky sleep pants was a jolt to his system. Not to mention the fact that her upper arms were sleekly muscled and tanned. Where did she get that tan?

"Do I really strike you as the kind of woman who would enjoy lounging on a beach for two weeks?"

"Yesterday," he told her, "I would have said no way. But today—" he paused and let his gaze sweep up and down the length of her in an appreciative glance "—maybe."

She seemed to realize what she was wearing and he thought he actually caught a flush of color fill her cheeks briefly. *Andi blushing?* How many more surprises could a man take?

"You should go," she said simply.

Yeah, he probably should. But not yet. He could see that she was nesting or some damn thing here and until she'd gotten it out of her system, nothing would budge her out of this tiny, unfinished house. So the quickest way to get things back to normal would be for him to help her. Besides, if he really had kept her so busy she couldn't even unpack over the past year, maybe he owed it to her.

Whether Andi knew it or not, she was going to be bored senseless with nothing more to do than paint and mow the yard and whatever the hell else needed doing around here. Her mind was too sharp, her organizational skills too well honed for her to be happy puttering around the house. The sooner she realized that, the better for all of them.

"Tell you what," he announced. "I'll take the next two weeks off, too."

"What? Why? What?" She shook her head as if she hadn't heard him clearly, and who could blame her?

Mac couldn't remember when he'd last taken time off. He'd always been reluctant to leave the business in anyone's hands but his own. Not even his vice president's, and there weren't many people Mac trusted more than Tim Flanagan.

Now, with both Mac and Andi out of the office, and Tim off investigating another possible business move, there'd be no one there but Laura and a couple of interns. But it wasn't as though he was leaving the country, he told himself. He was right here in Royal, so if Laura ran into problems, he was completely reachable. Besides, two weeks would be over in a blink and everything would get back to normal.

"You quit your job so you'd have time to do stuff like this, right?"

Andi's lips pursed for a second before she nodded. "In a nutshell, yes."

"Fine. Then I'll be here for the next two weeks, helping you slap this place into shape." He curled his fingers over the brim of his hat. "Once we're done, if you still want to quit, fine."

"I will," she told him. "In fact, I already *have* quit."

He shrugged. "You can always change your mind."

"Not going to happen."

"We'll just think of these next two weeks as a sort of trial period," he said as if she hadn't spoken at all. "You can see what it's like to be out of the office and still have a chance to call off your resignation."

"Mac, you're making this harder than it has to be."

Yeah, he thought, recognizing the stubborn set to her chin, the flash in her eyes. Her mind was set. But then, he reassured himself, so was his. And when Mac McCallum made a decision, it was set in stone. In short order, he was going to prove to Andi that she wasn't the kind of woman to walk away from a high-powered job. She liked the responsibility. Thrived on it.

He had no doubt at all who was going to come out the winner in their little contest of wills. And by the time Andi had spent two weeks doing nothing but nesting, she'd be yearning to get back to the office and dive right in.

Giving her a slow smile, he said, "Tomorrow morning, I'll go in, take care of a couple things, tie up some loose ends and then I'm all yours."

"Mine?"

His smile deepened. Maybe it was small of Mac, but he enjoyed seeing her confused and just a little flustered. That almost never happened. Andi was too controlled. Too organized. Too on top of every damn thing that entered her universe. Being able to throw her for a loop, he decided, was fun.

"Yeah," he said, hooking his thumbs in the front pockets of his jeans. "Like I said, I'll be here, helping you. So for the next two weeks, you're the boss and I'm the employee."

"I'm the boss?"

He winked. "Like the sound of that, don't you?"

While she stared at him, he shifted his gaze around the room, checking out the freshly painted walls. "You did a nice job in here—"

"Gee, thanks."

"—*but*," he added as if she hadn't spoken, "the ceiling could use another coat. Hard for you to reach it I guess, since you're not all that tall."

"I used a ladder—"

"I won't need one to go over it tomorrow. Then we'll do the trim."

"I don't want your help."

His gaze immediately locked on hers. "Maybe not. But you need it."

She opened her mouth, then shut it again and took a breath before speaking. "Mac, I appreciate the offer…"

"No, you don't." In fact, her storm-gray eyes were smoldering. Typical Andi—she'd never admit there was something she couldn't do on her own.

Her lips twitched. "Okay, no, I don't. But then, you don't really want to take time away from the office to paint my house, either."

Mac thought about it for a minute. Ordinarily no, he wouldn't. His company had been his life for so many years now, he couldn't really imagine taking two weeks away from it. But if he wanted to keep Andi working for him—and he did—then he'd have to invest the time to convince her to stay. So he shrugged off her comment as if it meant nothing. "When I was a kid, my dad had me out on the ranch painting the barn, the stables, the fence around my mother's garden. I'm damn good with a paintbrush. And at woodworking. The ranch carpenter taught me a lot back then. I've got a fair hand at plumbing, too, though that can be iffy."

"Why would you want to use your no doubt impressive skills on my house?"

Here he gave her a grin and a wink. "What kind of Texan would I be if I didn't ride to the rescue?"

Her head snapped back. "*Rescue?* I don't need to be rescued, Mac. And now's a good time to remind you that for the last six years, I'm the one who's done most of the rescuing."

He laughed. Her outrage put fire in her eyes and a rush of color in her cheeks. Her breath was coming fast and furious and her breasts hitched even higher beneath that skimpy tank top. He'd have to remember to make her furious more often.

"Okay," he said, "I'll give you that. You've been riding herd on the business and keeping things moving for six years. So now it's time I paid that back."

She shook her head. "I don't need you to pay me back for doing my job."

"Maybe it's not about what you need," he said, and felt tension crawl through him as he stared into her gray eyes, where the fire was now banked, simmering low. This woman had been a central part of his life for years and he wasn't ready for that to end yet. Now that he was here, with her, in this nearly empty house with the dark settling around them, he wanted that even less than when he'd first come here.

"We'll work together and at the end of two weeks, if you still want to walk away, so be it." Sounded reasonable, though Mac had no intention of letting her go. "This is my decision, Andi. And you should know better than anyone else, once I make a call, I stick to it."

A second or two passed before she blew out a breath. "You're impossible."

"You set this in motion, Andi," he told her, shaking his head. "I'm just riding your wave."

Until, he told himself, he could get her back to the office, where she belonged. In the end, he would have his way and his life and the office would get back to normal. He and Andi would be working together again. Because Mac McCallum never accepted less than exactly what he wanted.

She shouldn't have been nervous, but she was.

Andi got up the next morning and her stomach was a twist of knots in anticipation of Mac's arrival. Why was he making this so hard? Why couldn't he just accept her resignation and let her go? For six years he'd treated her as if she were nothing more than an efficient, invisible worker bee.

Why was he noticing her now?

Andi poured herself a cup of coffee and carried it out

to the front porch. She sat down on the top step, cradled her cup between her palms and stared out at the gnarled oaks and the fields that surrounded her small house. But her mind wasn't on the view. Instead, every thought she had was for Mac. He might think she'd change her mind and go back to work, but she wouldn't.

Yes, dealing with Mac when he was determined to do something was a little like being a wave pounding away at a boulder. But over time, she assured herself, water won. It wore the rock away until only the water remained.

So she would be a wave. Relentless. Taking a deep breath, she looked up at the wide sweep of deep blue sky and told herself that it was a good thing Mac was coming over. When he realized she wouldn't change her mind, they could both move on.

And, she didn't believe for a minute that he'd last the entire two weeks. But maybe while he *was* here, she could help him discover how to relax. Turn off his big brain and think about something other than McCallum Enterprises. The man had been working nonstop since he was a teenager and needed a break even more than she did. If she could help him find it while getting her house in shape, then she'd do it. It was one last thing she could do for him. She just hoped she'd survive having him so close and so out of reach all at the same time.

He showed up an hour later, dressed in battered jeans, a stained University of Texas T-shirt and the scarred, worn boots she knew he wore for working on the ranch. His dark blond hair ruffled in a hot breeze when he yanked his hat off and grinned at her. "Ready to work?"

What was it about the man's smile that could tangle

her stomach up into twisted threads of desire? Just that simple curve of his mouth was enough, though when it was matched with his deep voice and lazy way of speaking, he was her kryptonite.

"Ready?" she asked, lifting her coffee cup. "I'm on a break. Already started."

He winked and walked past her. "Then I'd best start catching up."

She followed him into the house, her gaze dropping unerringly to his butt, covered with soft, faded denim. Oh, this was such a bad idea.

"The living room needed another coat," she said, clearing her throat, "so I started in there."

"Yeah, I can see that." He tipped his head back, studied what she'd done so far and what still needed doing. Tossing his hat to the couch, he turned and asked, "Where's your roller? I'll get the ceiling and the walls while you cut in against the trim."

"Who put you in charge?"

He winked. "Honey, when a McCallum's around, they're just naturally in charge."

"Oh, for—" Irritating, yes, she admitted silently, but he made her laugh, too. He always had. She watched him pick up the roller with the extension pole and swipe it through a tray of paint. As much as it pained her to admit it, she really could use his help on the stupid ceiling. Her neck had hurt all night from straining and looking up for hours the day before.

He glanced over his shoulder at her and there was a knowing smile in his eyes. "So, you gonna start painting again or are you just going to stare at me?"

"Paint. I'm going to paint," she said firmly, not sure

if she was convincing him or herself. "Just go. Be in charge."

"Always easier when they acquiesce so quickly."

Andi snorted and deliberately ignored him as she started painting. It wasn't easy. She could *feel* him in the room. *Hear* him breathing her air. If she looked over her shoulder, would he be looking at her, too? Wow, she was way too old for these junior high school thoughts.

"It's a good color," he said, that deep voice of his reverberating in the room before rumbling up her spine.

She shrugged the sensation off and concentrated on laying down a wide path of paint. "Yeah, it feels cool and in summer, that'll help."

"You've got air conditioning, right?"

"Not yet," she admitted and sighed a little. It was already hot and she knew it was going to get ugly by afternoon. Last night had been a long, private misery. She'd kept her bedroom windows open, hoping a breeze would find its way in, but it hadn't helped.

"Bet it's number one on your list," he said.

"My list?" She turned to look at him.

He was grinning and his gaze fixed on her briefly as he said, "Andi, you make so many lists, you have a master list to keep track of them all."

Did he really know her that well? He turned back to work and probably didn't see evidence of the surprise that flickered inside her, then changed to something else the longer she watched him. Heat that had nothing to do with the weather pumped through her as she watched the play of muscles across his back and shoulders. Mac moved the roller smoothly, applying even swaths of paint with much more ease than she had the day before.

But it wasn't paint that interested her at the moment.

It was the man standing so close, so tall, so...*there*. Mesmerizing really, she thought, the ripple and flow of those muscles was just—

"Andi? Hey, you all right?"

She shook her head, forcing herself out of the hormonal stupor she'd slipped into. "What? Yes. Fine. What?"

He grinned and dipped the roller into the tray for more paint. "Daydreaming won't get the work done."

"Right." *Idiot.* Six years she'd worked with him and hadn't once betrayed anything she felt for him. Darned if she'd start now. She went to work, determined to concentrate on the task at hand.

"I asked if it was Bennet Heating and Cooling you called about the AC."

"Yes," she said, not bothering to turn around to look at him. "But they're backed up. It seems everyone in the county is getting their air worked on or installing new units. Won't get out here for a week or two."

He didn't answer, so she figured the conversation was over. Easier to keep her mind on painting when she could pretend he wasn't in the room with her, anyway. Then he started talking again—but not to her. Andi turned around to face him.

"Hey, Joe, it's Mac McCallum." He smiled at her and kept talking into his cell phone. "Yeah, I'm over at Andi Beaumont's place and she tells me you can't get out to install air conditioning for a week or two. That right?"

It was that whole "take charge" thing again. He couldn't seem to help himself. She started to tell him to butt out, but he actually held one finger up in the air in a sign for quiet. So Andi did a slow, silent burn.

"Yeah, that's not going to work for me. How about

you get your boys out here tomorrow? Damn hot in here and we're painting and fixing the place up." He winked at Andi then said more softly, "Now, Joe, I don't want to wait for this, understand me? I'd consider it a personal favor if you could handle this tomorrow."

Personal favor. Everyone in town was eager to do favors for Mac because he never forgot, and if Joe Bennet ever needed help down the line, Mac would be there to return the "favor."

Nodding, he said, "That's good news. I'll tell Andi you'll be here tomorrow then. Oh, and how about installing some of those new units where you don't need to put in all the duct work? Like you installed at my office? That way we get that puppy up and running soon as we can. Hotter than the halls of hell in here, Joe." Mac laughed, then nodded. "Good. Good, we'll see you then. Appreciate it."

He shut his phone off, stuck it in his pocket and said cheerfully, "There I go, rescuing you again."

"I didn't ask to be rescued," she reminded him.

"A good rescuer doesn't wait to be asked."

"You shouldn't have done that, Mac." He was rich, powerful and so damn likable with it, most people went along just because he'd charmed them. It was well-known in Royal that Mac McCallum got what he wanted when he wanted it, and as far as she knew, no one had ever told him no. At least, not for long.

His eyebrows lifted. "Want me to call him back, then? Tell him there's no hurry? You're fine with the heat?"

She bit down on her bottom lip. He had her and he knew it. No, she didn't need rescuing, but she'd be spiting herself if she turned down help when it was offered. What would she prove by doing that?

"No."

"Good."

"You still shouldn't have."

"You're welcome."

"I didn't say thank-you."

"I'm willing to look past that shameful lack of gratitude." He winked again. "And if I get a sandwich and some cold tea out of this deal I'll forgive you completely."

"You'll forgive *me*?" She choked out a laugh. "You're impossible."

"Can't be impossible," he said as he worked the paint roller smoothly. "Here I stand."

"The question is, why are you standing *here*?"

He lowered the roller, turned to look at her and said, "Because we're not done, Andi. I'm not willing to let you go, and I think over the next couple weeks we're both going to learn a thing or two."

Her stomach shivered and her mouth went dry. "If you really want to take time off—which is hard to believe— why not Paris? London? Jamaica?"

His eyes burned into hers. "You're not there, are you? Besides," he added, "why would I want to leave Texas?"

"You're making me a little crazy," she admitted, shaking her head.

"Nothing wrong with being a little crazy," he said. "It's the *lot* of crazy you have to watch out for."

He started painting again and Andi could only stare at him. He'd pretty much been the center of her business life for six years and now he was steamrolling his way through her personal life. Andi had deliberately taken these two weeks so she could get some space between herself and Mac.

How could she get over him if she was *with* him? But

she was forced to admit that she was glad she'd have two more weeks with him. It was probably foolish, but maybe while he was here, she really could help him find a way to relax. To turn off that sharp, brilliant mind long enough to enjoy his life a little. Except for the rare times when he went out on a date or two with some gorgeous yet dim model, actress or flight attendant, Mac was as relaxation-deprived as she was.

Then she remembered what Amanda had said only yesterday about *making* the time to have a secret lover in her life. She shot Mac a sidelong look and let her gaze sweep over him.

And suddenly, the next two weeks looked a lot more interesting.

Four

"Where have you been hiding the last few days?"

Mac looked across the table at one of his oldest friends. Rafiq "Rafe" bin Saleed no longer looked the part of a Harvard-educated sheikh. Between moving here to Royal and marrying Mac's sister, Vi, Rafe had been transformed into an honorary Texan.

Since he'd had to go by the office and take care of a couple of things—how did people go on vacations?— Mac had called Rafe to meet him at the Royal Diner. They were sharing a booth in the back, and Mac caught a couple of the other customers shooting them curious glances. He ignored them and lifted his coffee cup for a sip of the dark, hot brew.

"Thought for sure Vi would have told you. I've been at Andi's house, helping her put it together." He shrugged. "It's really why I called. I've spent most of my time here lately talking to no one but women. Andi. Laura. Your wife."

"Your sister," Rafe reminded him. "And why are you helping Andi fix up that old house?"

In that clipped, well-bred accent, the question sounded more demanding than inquisitory. Mac chuckled. "You may not be a sheikh anymore, but you've still got that do-as-I-say thing in your voice."

Rafe smiled and sipped at his own coffee. "I believe the correct phrase here would be 'it takes one to know one.'"

"Okay. Touché." Easing back in the booth, Mac glanced out the windows at Main Street. Shoppers hurried up and down the sidewalks, carrying bags and herding toddlers. Cars crawled along the street, mindful of the speed limit. Rivers of colorful flowers spilled from baskets hanging from the streetlights. It was Main Street, USA, out there—just the way Mac liked it.

"Did Vi tell you about Andi quitting her job?"

"She did." Rafe, too, looked out the window briefly before shifting his gaze back to his friend. "And that you're trying to change her mind. My friend, you should know that a woman is difficult to manage."

He snorted. "Manage? Nobody manages Andi." He admired that about her even as that personality trait was working against him at the moment. Grinning at Rafe, he said, "And I'd truly love to be there when Vi finds out you think you're *managing* her."

Rafe shivered. "A wise man never lets that information slip."

"True." While the diner filled with customers who went about their business, Mac looked at his old friend and took a moment to realize how glad he was that they had managed to put their friendship back together. "Off the fascinating subject of women for a minute," he said abruptly, "have you given any more thought to officially joining the Texas Cattleman's Club?"

"I have," Rafe said softly. "And I actually wanted to ask if you would be the one to support my application."

A wide, satisfied smile stretched across Mac's face as he held one hand out across the table. When Rafe took it in a hard, firm shake, Mac said, "My pleasure. Really."

"I appreciate that. It's good to be here with you like this, Mac." Rafe took a breath and let it out. "When I let myself think about what I almost lost, almost threw away, by refusing to see the truth—"

"Almost doesn't mean a damn, Rafe. What matters is that you did see it. Finally," he added, and laughed when his friend winced at the reminder. "I'm glad to have you back, too. Plus, you married my sister, you poor dumb fool…"

"She's wonderful and you know it."

"Yeah," Mac allowed. "But don't tell her I said so." Shaking his head again, he said, "Wish to hell Andi was as easy to read as Violet."

"I wouldn't say your sister is 'easy' to understand."

Mac brushed that comment aside. "But Andi's always been easy to be around. She's a hell of a taskmaster. Kept the business running without a bump for years. Hell, Rafe, I thought I *knew* her. And all of a sudden, she's turned everything around on me. I feel like this is a woman I don't know at all."

"Maybe you don't," Rafe mused. "A work relationship is entirely different from life on the outside."

"Yeah, but people are who they are."

"Not always. When you're not wheeling and dealing,

you like being on a horse and speaking as if you're in an old Western movie."

Mac snorted. "Why was I glad to see you again?"

"Because everyone needs an honest friend." Rafe lifted his coffee cup in a salute.

"Maybe. And maybe you're right, too, about the work thing. Andi's determined to quit, damn it, and I can't let that happen."

"It may be that you won't be able to stop it."

Mac shot him a hard look. "Whose side are you on?"

Rafe held up both hands in mock surrender. "Yours, my friend. Of course. But as I have learned in dealing with your sister, I can say that a woman's mind is a tricky, always evolving thing."

"So I've noticed." He took another drink of coffee.

"And I've noticed," Rafe said with a cautious glance around, "that some in Royal are still unsure about me."

Mac sighed a little. "Well, this is one of the reasons I wanted you to meet me here. The more people see us together, as friends, the more they'll move on from what happened before. They'll all figure out that the hatchet's been buried and there's no hard feelings. Folks in Royal aren't the type to hold grudges, Rafe. They'll get past it—just like I did."

Rafe smiled. "Thank you for that, my friend. With you and Violet on my side, I'm sure all will be well."

"Wish I was as sure of my own situation as I am of yours," Mac said.

"How are my two most handsome customers doing?" Amanda Battle walked up to their table and gave each of them a wide smile.

"Coffee's good and so's the ambience," Mac said, smiling back.

"It's what I like to hear," Amanda said. "Now, Rafe, you tell Violet I expect her to come around soon. I want to keep an eye on that baby bump of hers."

"I will do it," he agreed, pleasure shining in his dark eyes.

"As for you," Amanda said, giving Mac a wink, "you tell Andi I said to remember that 'secret' we were talking about."

"Okay," Mac said warily.

She gave them their check, told them to hurry back, then walked away to say hello to more of her customers.

"Now, what do you suppose that was about?" Mac asked. "What 'secret'?"

"I have already said, my friend," Rafe told him as he picked up the check and headed for the cash register. "A woman's mind is a tricky and evolving thing."

"Yeah," Mac muttered as he followed his friend. "Just what I need. Tricky women with secrets."

For the next couple of days, Mac and Andi worked together on the old house. The amount of renovation that still needed to be done was staggering, though, and Mac had a twinge or two of guilt a couple times. It was because of him and his business that Andi hadn't had time to take care of her house before. But he didn't let regret take too big a chunk out of him because damned if he'd feel bad for hiring her, handing over responsibilities and coming to count on her for too damn much.

If she hadn't wanted to become irreplaceable, then she shouldn't have been so good at her job.

"She's not walking away. Not from the office. Not from *me*," he swore quietly. He'd figure out a way past all of this. It was what he did.

He'd still like to know what "secret" Amanda Battle had been talking about. Especially because when he'd mentioned it to Andi, she'd blushed a fiery red and smiled to herself. And if that wasn't enough to make a man wonder, he didn't know what would. But she'd refused to tell him, and just got to work stripping old wallpaper off the dining room walls so they, too, could be painted.

Now while she was in there, here he was, head and shoulders under her first-floor powder room sink. When Mac had arrived, she was about to call a plumber to fix a leaking pipe and he'd insisted on doing it himself. If she needed help then he'd damn well provide it. He was going to make himself as irreplaceable to her as she was to him.

Mac wielded a pipe wrench on the joist that was tight enough to have been welded on, and when the damn wrench slipped free, he scraped his knuckles on the old copper pipes. He hissed in a breath and let it go on a string of muffled curses. Then he jolted when his cell phone rang and rapped his head on the underside of the sink and briefly saw stars. Cursing a bit louder now, he wiggled out, reached for the phone and muttered, "What?"

"Hey, boss, good talking to you, too."

Reaching up, Mac rubbed the growing knot on top of his head then glared at the raw scrape on his knuckles. "Tim. What's going on?"

Tim Flanagan, a friend since college, was now Mac's vice president. He was currently in Montana going over the details of a ranch takeover. The Gilroy ranch was being swallowed by McCallum Enterprises and would soon be stocked with prime cattle.

"I called the office looking for you," Tim said. "Laura

told me you haven't been in for a few days." He paused. "Somebody die?"

Snorting, Mac shook his head, drew one knee up and rested his forearm on it. His gaze shot around the incredibly tiny first-floor powder room. Whoever the last owner had been, they'd painted it a dark brick red, making the room seem even smaller than it actually was. And to top it off, they'd used gold paint for the trim. It looked as if it belonged in a bordello. Not a particularly exclusive one, either. Naturally, Andi had plans for it, but first thing was getting the plumbing working right—such as making it so the sink would drain.

"Yeah, nobody's dead. I'm taking a few days is all." He rested his head against the bottom of the old sink and let the cool of the porcelain seep into his body. Thanks to the newly installed air conditioning, he wasn't dying of heat, but a man could still work up a sweat when wrestling with stubborn pipes.

"I heard Andi quit," Tim said. "What's up with that?"

Mac shot a glance out the door to make sure the woman in question wasn't in earshot. Then he said, "I'm working on it."

"Good," Tim told him with a slight laugh. "Because without her as a buffer I probably would have killed you five, six years ago."

Mac's mouth twitched in a smile. "You would have tried. So, is there some reason in particular you're calling or was it just to harass me?"

"There's a reason. Harassment's just a bonus. Old man Gilroy's wanting to hold back ten acres, claiming it's in the contract for him to get the allowance for a hay field."

Frowning now, Mac said, "I don't remember it that way." They'd made allowances for the Gilroy ranch house and the surrounding five acres to remain in their name, as a courtesy since the Gilroys had been on the land more than a hundred years.

But the truth was, the old man couldn't run the ranch on his own anymore and his kids weren't interested in being ranchers. They loved the land and wanted at least some of it to remain in the family, but the younger Gilroys all had jobs that took them off the ranch. McCallum Enterprises was paying fair market value for the land and Mac wasn't about to hand out favors. That just wasn't how you ran a business.

"Call the office, have Laura pull up the contract and get the details," Mac said. "We want to be sure of our standing here and—"

"What's going on?" Andi stepped into the doorway and leaned one shoulder against the jamb.

Mac looked up at her and damn, she looked good. No woman should look as fine when she'd been ripping away at dirty old wallpaper. He gave his head a shake, reminding himself to focus, then told Tim to hang on and explained, "Tim says Mr. Gilroy in Montana is insisting that we agreed to an extra ten acres set aside for him in the contract and I don't—"

"You did," she said, then reached down and plucked the phone from his hand. "Hi, Tim, it's Andi. The original contract called for just the house and the surrounding five acres to remain in Gilroy hands. But we renegotiated several points about two weeks into the deal and Mac agreed to a ten-acre plot behind the main ranch house. Mr. Gilroy wants his daughter and her husband to be able to build near the main house. And they want to grow enough hay for the animals they're keeping."

Mac watched her. She had pulled that information out

of her computerlike brain, and damned if he didn't find that sexy as hell. A woman with a mind like that didn't waste herself. She needed challenge. Needed the kind of work she'd been doing for six years. Why the hell did she think she could be happy without it?

"Sure," Andi said and grinned. "It's no problem, Tim. Happy to help. Okay, here's Mac again."

She handed him back the phone. "Problem solved."

"Yeah," he said, still watching her. "I see that. You always were impressive."

"Thanks." She left a second later but he continued to look after her. Then he spoke into the phone. "Everything straightened out now?"

"Yeah," Tim said. "She is *good.* With all the things we have going on concurrently, it amazes me that she could just remember details like that. What the hell are we going to do without her?"

Mac shifted his gaze to the ceiling when he heard her footsteps pass overhead. He wondered briefly what she was doing up there. Then he realized that if she left, he'd spend the rest of his life wondering what she was up to. That was unacceptable. "We're never gonna have to find out."

Two hours later, Andi set two sandwiches on her tiny kitchen table and poured two tall glasses of iced tea. If it felt odd serving Mac lunch, she brushed it off, knowing that with all the work he'd done around there the past few days, the least she owed him was a meal.

He walked into the kitchen and grinned at her. "I didn't even know you could cook."

"A ham and cheese sandwich is not cooking," she said, and took a seat. Picking up a potato chip, she bit in and chewed. "However, I'm a darn good cook—when I have the time."

He winced and sat down opposite her at the table. "Time again. Point made."

She shrugged and smiled. "It's not all you and the job," she admitted as she looked around the room. "This kitchen is not exactly conducive to creative cookery. Plus, the oven doesn't work."

He looked behind him and laughed. "A pink stove?"

"It might come back in style," she said, not sure why she was bothering to defend the appliance she had every intention of replacing. When he just gave her a you've-got-to-be-kidding look, she said, "Fine. It's terrible. But getting a new one is low on my list right now. Anyway, you bought pizza yesterday, so it's only fair I take care of lunch today."

"Always about what's fair, aren't you?"

"Something wrong with that?"

"Not a thing," he assured her and picked up half his sandwich. "But if you're so fired up about being 'fair' you might want to rethink walking out on a business that needs you."

Andi watched him, and though she felt that rush of knowing he didn't want to lose her, she knew it was still the only answer for her. Being around him so much the past few days had been so hard. Her heart ached for what she couldn't have, and if she stayed working for him, that ache would eventually swallow her whole.

"You were doing fine before me and you'll do fine without me," she said, taking a bite herself.

"Fine's one thing," he said, waving his sandwich at her. "Great's another. And you know damn well that together, we were doing great."

"There's more to life than work, Mac." At least she hoped there was. And she fully intended to find out.

"If you love what you do, you'll never work a day in your life. My dad told me that when I was a kid," Mac said. "Someone famous said it, I think. Anyway, turns out Dad was right. Work is *fun*, Andi, and you know it."

She had enjoyed her job, keeping on top of problems, working out strategies and plans for the future. It was exciting and fulfilling and everything a good career should be. But to be honest, doing all of that *with Mac* was what had really been the best part for her.

With his free hand, he pulled his phone out of his shirt pocket and scrolled through, checking email. Andi shook her head. Even during lunch, he couldn't stop working. "This is exactly what I'm talking about."

"Huh? What?" He didn't look at her. Instead, he tapped out an answer, hit Send, then checked for incoming texts and missed calls.

"Look at you. You can't even stop working long enough to eat a sandwich."

"Multitasking," he argued, shooting her a quick look. "Contrary to what women believe, men are capable of doing more than one thing at once. Besides, I'm just—"

Before he could finish, she interrupted. "Twenty dollars says you can't go an hour without checking your phone."

"What?" His cool green eyes shone with bemusement.

"It's a bet, Mac." She braced her forearms on the table and gave him a rueful smile.

"Yeah, I know that," he said, setting the phone at his elbow. "But I don't feel right about taking your money."

His phone vibrated and he glanced at the readout. When he looked back at her, her eyebrows were arched and there was a definite smirk on her mouth. "Oh, I think my money's safe enough. Especially since I don't think you'll take the bet, because you know you'd lose."

Frowning, he picked up the phone and tapped out an answer to the text from Laura. "I've got a business to run, you know."

"That's *all* you've got, Mac," she said as he set the phone aside again. "It's all I had until I quit."

His mouth tightened and she watched a muscle in his jaw twitch as if he had plenty to say but was holding the words back.

It took a couple of seconds, but he finally put his sandwich down, tipped his head to one side and asked, "And you really believe you had to walk out to find more?"

"Yeah." She took a sip of her tea because her throat was suddenly dry and tight. "Look at you. You said you were going to be here, working on the house for two weeks. But you haven't really left the office at all."

He grabbed a chip, tossed it into his mouth and crunched viciously. "What's that supposed to mean?"

"It means that you can take the boy out of the office, but you can't take the office out of the boy." She shook her head, sad to realize that she'd been right to leave. Mac didn't need a woman in his life. He had his *work*. "All the while you're painting or fixing the broken tiles or unclogging a sink, you're checking your phone. Answering emails. Texts. Checking with Laura about the situation at the office."

"What's wrong with that?"

"Nothing if it's all you want. Heck, until I quit, I was doing the same thing." Andi looked down at her own empty hands and said, "I was almost convinced my phone was an extension of my hand. Every waking moment revolved around the business and all of the minutiae involved with keeping it running. It was getting crazy, Mac. I was practically *showering* with my phone. That's when it hit me that not only did I want more, but I *deserved* more. And you do, too."

"This is all because I check my phone?"

"Because you can't *stop* checking your phone."

It vibrated on the table again and instinctively he started to reach for it—then stopped, curling his fingers into his palm. He locked his gaze with hers. "Twenty bucks?"

"Only if you can go an entire hour without checking your phone—or responding to a call." He'd never be able to do it, Andi told herself. Right now, she could see it was *killing* him to not answer whoever had called or texted.

He thought about it for a long moment, then seemed to come to a decision. "You're on, but first—" he hedged as he picked up his phone "—I send one text to Laura telling her to go to Tim with any questions."

Andi met his gaze and nodded. "Agreed. But after that, it's one hour. No phone."

Mac texted Laura at the office, put the phone in his pocket and held out one hand to her. "Deal."

The instant his hand closed around hers, Andi felt a rush of heat that raced up her arm to settle in the middle of her chest. As if he, too, felt that zip of something wicked, he held on to her hand a little longer than necessary. She couldn't look away from his eyes. The sharp, cool green of them drew her in even when she knew she should resist the fall. With the touch of his hand against hers, though, it was so hard to think about caution.

When he finally let her go, Andi could still feel the

warmth of his skin, and clasped her hands together in her lap to hang on to that feeling as long as she could.

"What do I get when I win?" he asked.

Was it her imagination or was his voice deeper, more intimate than it had been only a moment ago? Quickly, she picked up her glass of tea and took a long drink before answering.

"The prize is twenty dollars. But you won't win."

"Uh-huh." One corner of his mouth curved up and Andi tightened her grip on the tea glass in response.

"When I win," he said, "I'm going to need a little more than a paltry twenty dollars."

She swallowed hard. "Is that right?"

"Oh, yeah." He picked up his sandwich again and gave her a teasing smile over it.

Well, when Mac's eyes gleamed like that, Andi knew he had something up his sleeve. Over the years, she'd watched him back opponents into corners or wheedle exactly what he wanted out of a deal in spite of the odds being against him. And it was always heralded by that smile.

So warily, she asked, "What did you have in mind?"

"Well, now," he mused, taking another bite, "I believe that after this amazing sandwich, we're going to be needing dinner."

"And?" she prompted.

"And, the two of us. Dinner. The club."

"The TCC?" she asked, surprised.

Mac, like his father before him, was a member of the Texas Cattleman's Club, a members-only private organization that had only recently begun to welcome women as full members. The club was legendary in Royal, with most people going their whole lives and never seeing the inside of the place. "Why would you want to do that?"

"They serve a great steak," he said with a careless shrug that she didn't believe for a minute.

Whatever his reasons for suggesting they go out on a real dinner date—he was suggesting a *date*, wasn't he? Oh, God, why was he asking her on a date? Because he knew he'd never have to go through with it, that's why, she thought an instant later. He couldn't win this bet and he knew it.

"Okay," she said, agreeing in the same spirit he'd asked. "Deal. Dinner at the TCC if you win. Which you won't."

"Seem awful sure of yourself," he mused.

"You'll never be able to go without answering your phone," she said, taking a bite of her sandwich.

"Never say never, darlin'."

Five

The first half hour just about drove him out of his mind. He couldn't count how often he actually went to reach for his phone before stopping himself just in time. Whenever his phone rang, Andi watched him, one eyebrow lifted high as she waited for him to surrender to the inevitable. But he didn't do it. Mostly because she was so sure he would and that just annoyed the hell out of him. So he held out and poured his concentration into painting, and humming along with the country tunes on the radio.

He and Andi talked and worked together as well as they always had, and before Mac knew it, three hours had gone by. He hadn't checked his phone once, he realized, and the world hadn't ended. His business was still up and running and there were no signs of a coming apocalypse. Even more than that—after the first agonizing half hour, he'd actually enjoyed not grabbing for the phone whenever it beeped or vibrated.

"You did it," Andi said, with just a hint of surprised admiration in her voice. "I didn't think you'd make it, but you did."

"You should have learned by now not to doubt me," he said, taking a step back to survey the job they'd done. "Looks good, Andi."

"It does," she said, turning in a circle to admire the room now that it was finished. "We make a good team."

"Always did," he agreed, then kept talking before she could back away from that one simple truth. "So, if it's okay with you, think I'll use my phone now and make us a reservation at the TCC. Then I'll use that twenty bucks you owe me to put gas in my truck."

Her head tipped to one side. "You want to have dinner with me?"

"I guess I do." He wanted a lot more than dinner, too. But a man had to start somewhere. He pulled his phone from his pocket and hit the speed dial. When she started to speak again, he held up one finger for quiet and watched her quietly steam. It was probably wrong how much he enjoyed doing that.

"Afternoon, James. This is Mac McCallum. I'll be bringing a guest in for dinner tonight. Around eight. Thanks. Appreciate it." He hung up and looked at her. "They're holding my favorite table."

"Of course they are."

"Problem?" he asked.

"You always get what you want, don't you?"

"Damn straight."

"I shouldn't even be surprised when people snap to attention when you speak, should I?"

"I've never seen you jump when I speak," he said.

Her mouth curved. "True."

"Always liked that about you," he admitted. That stiffness in her spine, the determined gleam in her eyes and the defiant tilt to her chin all rolled together to make her one amazing woman. "From that first day you came in to interview for the job. You let me know from the start that you'd work your butt off, but you wouldn't be a yes woman."

"You didn't need one more person kowtowing to you."

Amusement filled him. "Kowtow?"

"It's an appropriate word."

His eyebrows lifted as he considered it. He supposed she had a point, in spite of that snotty tone. However everyone else treated him, Andi had always given him an honest opinion. No matter what. He had always known that she'd tell him straight and wouldn't hold back. And he was only now seeing how much he'd come to rely on that trait over the years.

He could still see her as she had been that first day. He'd interviewed three people for the job before her, but the moment she walked into the office, all starch and precision, he'd known she would be the one. She'd had a great résumé, a firm demeanor and he liked how she had stood right up to him.

Now she wanted to leave. Was it any wonder he was trying so hard to keep her?

He studied her for a second or two, and in her eyes he saw more than his trusted assistant. More than the woman who'd made his work life run like a Swiss watch. He saw a woman he enjoyed being around. A woman who made his skin sizzle with a touch and irritated him and intrigued him all at once. Why had he never opened his eyes to the possibilities before this?

Looked as though he was just going to have to make up for lost time.

"So," he said, cutting his own thoughts off. "Dinner tonight. I'll pick you up at eight."

He looked at her steadily, silently daring her to say no. Just when it seemed she might, she said, "Fine. Eight."

Nodding, Mac started talking again before she could change her mind. "I'll finish with this sink, then head home to clean up, take care of some things."

She was standing close. So close he could smell her shampoo. Why had he never noticed that soft, flowery scent before? Her T-shirt was tight, clinging to her breasts and her narrow waist. Her cutoff denim shorts were cuffed high on her thighs and those pale pink toes looked too damn sexy.

His breath labored in his lungs, and every square inch of his body tightened until he felt as if a giant fist was wrapped around him, squeezing. They stared at each other for several long seconds, and then Andi broke away, shattering whatever thread had been stretched between them. Mac took a deep breath, thinking to settle himself, but all it did was make him appreciate her scent that much more.

"Um, okay then. I'll get back to the hideous cabbage rose wallpaper and—" She half turned and he stopped her.

"Wait," he said tightly. She tensed up. He could see it and he enjoyed knowing that she was feeling as twisted up as he was. Reaching out, he pulled flakes of wallpaper out of her hair, then held them out to her with a smile.

"Isn't that perfect?" she muttered. Taking them, her fingers brushed against his and sent another quick snap of sensation between them. "Thanks. I'll be sure to wash my hair before dinner."

Well, now he was imagining her in the shower, soap suds and water running over her bare skin, hair slicked back from her flushed face to hang down her back in heavy, wet strands… Oh, man. He rubbed one hand across his mouth, hoping he wasn't drooling.

She gave him a long look out of those storm-gray eyes that had his insides fisting. He fought down an urge to grab her, pull her close and hold on to her. Because if he held her, he'd have to kiss her. Taste the mouth that was suddenly more tempting to him than anything he'd ever seen before. But if he did that, it would change their relationship completely and, knowing her, Andi would only use that shift between them as another reason to leave her job. So he wouldn't risk it. Not yet, anyway.

When she turned to the hall, this time he let her go.

"A date? Seriously? You're going on a date with Mac?"

Jolene and the kids had stopped by on their way home from baseball practice and now Andi and her sister were sitting in the kitchen, keeping an eye on Jacob, Jilly and Jenna playing in the backyard. She had less than two hours before Mac picked her up for their not-a-date.

"It's not a date," Andi insisted, as she had been telling herself all afternoon.

"Really?" Jolene reached out and tapped her fingernail against the window until her son looked up. She wagged her finger at him and Jacob got the message, immediately letting go of his baby sister's doll. The little girl's shrieks broke off instantly. Satisfied, Jolene turned back to Andi.

"If it's not a date, what's the word they use to describe it these days?"

"Funny," Andi told her. She sliced a couple of apples into wedges, then added squares of cheese to a plate before carrying it all to the table and sitting down opposite her sister. "Really, I don't know what it is. But he's never thought about me *that* way, so I know it's not a date."

"Uh-huh." Jolene took a sip of her tea and flicked another glance out the window to make sure no one was killing anybody. "Sounds to me like he's thinking of you 'that' way now."

"No, he's not. Is he?" She worried her bottom lip as she considered, then rejected the whole idea. "No, he's not."

"Things change," Jolene said, snatching a slice of apple and crunching into it. "Let us pause to remember that after my first date with my beloved Tom I told him I never wanted to see him again."

"That's because he took you fly-fishing."

"He really was an idiot," Jolene murmured with a smile. Rubbing one hand over her belly, she said, "But look at us now."

"Okay, you have a point. Things have already changed." In the past few days, there had been a kind of *shift* in her relationship with Mac. Always before, they'd been friendly, but she'd been determined to maintain that cool separation of boss and assistant. But here, away from the office, that barrier had dropped and they'd both reached across it.

What that meant, she had no idea.

"What're you going to wear?" Jolene asked.

"Oh, God." She dropped her head to the table and only groaned when her sister laughed.

* * *

Andi swiveled her head from side to side and didn't even care that she must look like a tourist on their first visit to New York City. It was how she felt. She'd never been inside the Texas Cattleman's Club before, so this was a real moment for her. She didn't want to miss a thing—and not only because Jolene had demanded a full description.

The building itself was stone and wood and boasted a tall slate roof that afforded the rooms in the club with nearly-cathedral ceilings. The paneled walls were dotted with hunting trophies and pieces of the history of Royal, Texas. Old photos of stern-looking men glaring at the camera were interspersed with other Texas memorabilia. Andi took it all in as Mac led her toward the dining room.

"I feel like we should have had to use a secret password to get in here," she said, keeping her voice low as if she were in a library.

"Ah, we use code signals. Much more stealthy." He leaned his head toward hers. "Did you see how I tipped my hat to the right when I took it off? There you go."

Her lips twitched. A playful Mac was a dangerous Mac. At least to her heart. "This is exciting. To finally see it all."

Mac tucked her arm through his. "Well, the dancing girls are only here Tuesdays and Thursdays, and the harem's closed to female guests, so you'll have to make do with the dining room."

She tipped her head up to give him a sardonic look. "Aren't you the funny one?"

"Charm, Andi. It's called charm."

"There's a less attractive name for it, as well," she told him.

He laughed. "You're quick. I like it. Always did. So what do you think of the place?"

"I feel like we should be whispering," she confessed, lowering her voice again as she looked at the old framed letters on her left and nearly gasped when she saw one signed by Sam Houston himself.

"The place has got plenty of history," he said, "but it's moving with the times, too."

She raised an eyebrow at that.

"Okay, turtle speed," he allowed. "But we are moving. We even have a day care center here now and I thought that was going to send a couple of the older members into heart attacks."

She chuckled, but realized he was probably right. The arguments over the day care center had kept the town talking for weeks. But oh, she remembered well how infuriated the old guard of the club had been to grudgingly accept female members.

In a way, she felt sort of sorry for the poor old dinosaurs. Their world was changing and they couldn't stop it.

"Of course," Mac was saying as he shifted his gaze to the ceiling, "the building suffered some damage during the tornado. But I like what they did when they repaired it. There's a little more light in here—makes it seem less like a paneled cave when you walk through."

"I love it." She tipped her head back to look up at him. "I've always had a mental image of what the inside of this place might look like and, surprisingly enough, I was pretty close. But you've fulfilled a childhood dream by bringing me here. So thank you."

"Absolutely my pleasure," he assured her. Then he covered her hand on his arm with his own. The closeness to him was exhilarating and made her head swim. She liked it.

He looked wonderful, though she had to admit that he always looked far too good. Tonight, he wore black slacks, black boots, a white collared shirt and a black jacket. He carried his black dress Stetson in his free hand and his sharp green eyes surveyed every inch of his surroundings.

He *fit* in this building that was so much a combination of past and present. She could completely see Mac McCallum a hundred and fifty years ago, still having that steely gaze, carving out an empire in the Old West.

As if he felt her watching him, he turned his head, looked down into her eyes and asked, "What's going on in your mind right now?"

"Too many things I don't want to talk about."

"Intriguing."

She sighed a little. "I'm not trying to be intriguing."

"Maybe that's why you are," he said, voice low, a caress of sound in the hushed atmosphere. Well, that should keep her system humming for a while, she thought as he led her into the main dining room.

Here, the tables were square, covered in white linen then draped with deep red cloths. There were candles and tall, fragile vases, each holding a single yellow rose. It made her smile.

Leaning toward him, she whispered, "The yellow rose of Texas?"

He grinned, as if pleased she'd caught it. "Nobody has traditions like Texas."

She'd been so nervous about coming here with him,

worried about what it might mean, what would happen. And now she was enjoying herself too much. It wasn't good, she thought. She couldn't allow her feelings for him to keep growing. If she did, walking away would be even harder than it had to be.

"Stop thinking."

Andi blinked and shook her head as if coming up out of a trance. "What?"

"I can see you're starting to second-guess tonight." Mac dropped one hand to the small of her back. "Why not just let it roll on and see where it takes us instead?"

Ignoring the burst of warmth that bloomed from his touch, she sat down and kept her gaze on his as he took the seat beside her at the table for four. "You hired me for my organizational skills, for my ability to think everything through from every angle."

"As you're continually reminding me," he said with a quick smile, "we're not at work."

If they were, Andi would know where she stood. As it was now, she felt a little off balance—a not altogether uncomfortable feeling.

"Right. Okay. Just enjoy." She looked around the dining room. There were several other people at the tables scattered across the gleaming wood floor. She recognized most of them and nodded to Joe Bennet, who excused himself to his wife and headed across the room toward them.

He and Mac shook hands, then Joe turned to Andi and asked, "How's that new air conditioning system I installed working out for you?"

Here she had no trouble knowing exactly what to say. Giving him a wide smile, she said, "It's wonderful, Joe.

I can't thank you enough. It's lovely being able to sleep at night without gasping for air."

His wide, plain face beamed with pleasure. "Happy to hear it. Now, if you have any problems at all, you let me know, all right?"

"I will."

"You enjoy your night, you two." He gave Mac a conspiratorial wink, then walked back to his own table.

"Oh, boy." That man-to-man wink was a sure sign that she and Mac were about to be the hot topic of conversation tomorrow in Royal.

"Yeah," Mac said, nodding. "I know what you mean. Joe's a good guy, but the man gossips like an old woman. Did you know he spent a half hour telling me how the Grainger boy's scholarship to UT came at the right time. His dad was so proud he forgot all about the boy crashing the family car."

"Did he?" Amused, Andi listened.

"And when he'd finished with that tale, he moved right on to Sylvia Cooper and how her husband, Buck, bought her a shiny new cast-iron skillet for their twenty-fifth anniversary—and she promptly bounced it off his forehead."

She cringed. "Oh!"

"Yeah," he said with a wince. "Have to say, though, I think Buck had that one coming. Anyway, twenty stitches and a mild concussion later, Buck saw the light, bought two tickets to Paris and the lovebirds leave next week."

Andi laughed, enjoying herself as Mac continued.

"Then Joe went on a rant about Pastor Stevens and how he preaches against gambling but made a bet on a horse race last Friday night and won—without telling his old friend Joe about the tip he got before the race."

She was having fun. Andi hadn't expected to, not really. There was too much tension between them.

The quiet of the restaurant, the efficient smoothness of the waiters moving from table to table and the intimacy of the candlelight flickering in his eyes made her want to hug this moment close. Watching his easy smile slide across his face had her returning it and saying, "So Joe's a big gossip, is he?"

Mac laughed, then shrugged off the obvious dig. "Must be contagious."

"I think it is," she agreed and looked around at the people shooting them interested glances. "And by tomorrow afternoon, everyone in town will know we were out to dinner together."

"That bothers you?"

Her shoulder blades itched as though people were staring. "I don't like being talked about."

He laughed again and the sound was low and deep. "Don't know how you could avoid it around here. You know how it is in small towns. You've lived in Royal all your life just like me."

True, they had grown up just a few miles apart, but their lives were so different they could have been on separate planets. Mac had been the golden boy. Football team captain, star baseball player. His parents were wealthy, he lived on one of the biggest ranches in the state and everything he touched turned to gold. Until his parents died, leaving him to care for Violet and find his own way alone.

Andi and Jolene had grown up in town, in a nice middle-class home with two parents who doted on them and loved each other. She and her sister had worked hard at after-school jobs, not leaving much time for activities like cheerleading or drill team or band.

So, though they had both grown up here, and she had of course known who Mac was, Andi had never met him until the day she applied for a job with his company. She'd thought she'd come to know him very well over the years, but the past few days had shown her a new side of him, and it was fascinating to discover there was still so much more of him to know.

He was staring at her as if he could delve into her mind and read her every thought. Just in case he could, she spoke up quickly. "Vi seems really happy."

Mac nodded as if accepting her change of subject. "She is. Rafe loves her, which I'm grateful for, as I'd hate to have to pound on one of my best friends. And right now, she's driving the poor guy nuts with trying to get the nursery ready for the baby."

"He's loving it and you know it," Andi said.

"Okay, he is. It's only me she's driving nuts."

The waiter arrived, took their order and Andi listened as once again Mac took charge. She gave him this one, since, being a Texan, she liked a good steak now and then. The wine he ordered was served a few minutes later and, after being sampled, was poured. Then the two of them were alone again and she took a long sip of that wonderful red, just to ease the twisting knots in her stomach.

"Do you spend a lot of time here at the club?" she asked.

Mac winked. "Lately, it's been pointed out to me repeatedly that the only place I spend a *lot* of time is at work…"

She nodded at his implication.

"But yes," he said, glancing around the dark, intimate dining room. With a shrug, he added, "Food's good. If I want company, it's here, if I don't, I get left alone. Not much point in making Teresa dirty up the kitchen at home cooking just for me."

His housekeeper, Teresa Mooney, was a fifty-year-old widow who, Andi guessed, would love to be allowed to fuss over her employer. But typically enough, Mac made that call for her, not bothering to find out how she felt about it.

"You do that a lot, you know?" she said.

"What's that?"

"Make decisions for people."

"What're you talking about?"

"I ran into Teresa at the grocery store a few weeks ago. She was looking at a huge pot roast and bemoaning the fact that you don't want her to cook for you."

"Really?" He frowned a little, took a sip of wine.

"Yes, really." Andi sighed. "People like to feel needed. Useful. You're taking that away from her."

"Bad analogy," he said, shaking his head. "*You* felt needed and useful at the office and yet you walked away."

She shifted uneasily in her chair. "That's different."

"Not so much," he said, drinking his wine, then thoughtfully staring at her over the rim of the glass. "You're leaving *because* you were needed."

"It's not only that."

"Then what else?"

Okay, she wasn't about to admit that she'd left because she loved him and knew her dreams were doomed to die. "It doesn't matter," she said, evading the question she couldn't answer.

"Well," he said, setting his glass down as their meal arrived, "once you're back in the office where you belong, I'll have plenty of time to find out what's really bothering you."

She glanced up at the waiter and smiled as he served her dinner, waiting until the man was gone again to speak. When she did, she leaned in close enough that Mac could hear her whisper, "You're not going to convince me to come back."

"You didn't think I'd win our bet today either, but here we are." Smiling to himself, he cut into his steak.

Andi sat there quietly simmering, wondering just when it was she'd lost control of the situation. She'd quit her job, yet now she was half convinced that Mac was right. He would find a way to get her back.

Six

Mac didn't want the night to end yet—though he wasn't interested in asking himself why. It was enough to keep her with him awhile longer. After dinner, he coaxed her into taking a walk down Main Street. With the summer just getting started, the night was warm, but the breeze was cool and just strong enough to lift the hem of the dark red dress she wore and flutter it above her knees.

He was forced to admit that he'd felt staggered from the moment he picked her up at her house tonight. Over the past few days, Mac had been seeing Andi in a whole new light and it was just a little disconcerting. And tonight, she'd kicked it up several notches.

She had her hair pulled back at the sides so that it tumbled down her back in a waving mass that tempted a man to sink his hands into it. Her red dress had thin, narrow straps and a bodice that dipped low enough that he got another peek at the breasts she had apparently been hiding from him for six years. The fabric then nipped in at a waist so narrow he was willing to bet he could encircle it with his hands, then sloped down over rounded hips and clung there, just to torment him further. Not to mention, he thought with an inner groan, the heels. Black, shiny, four inches at least, with a cut-out toe that showed off the dark red polish on her nails.

She'd practically killed him right there on her front porch.

Every man at the club had watched her pass by and for the first time ever jealousy stirred through Mac. He'd never been possessive about a woman. Never cared if other men looked at her or even if she looked back. Until now. Admitting that to himself was damned unsettling.

At work, she had always been the personification of professionalism. Tidy, businesslike, she'd never once hinted at the woman beneath the veneer, and right now he figured that was a good thing. If she had, he might have fired her so he could date her and would never have been able to appreciate what she could bring to the business. And now, he thought, work was the furthest thing from his mind.

Her scent wafted to him on a sigh of wind and he inhaled it deeply, drawing it into him until he could practically taste her. Which was just what he wanted to do.

"It's a pretty little town, isn't it?" she asked when they got back to the car. She'd turned to look back down Main, and the expression on her face was soft and dreamy.

He turned to face the town he'd grown up in and saw it as she did. Street lamps formed globes of yellow light that were reflected in puddles on the sidewalk. Tubs and hanging baskets of flowers brightened the scene and the shop windows were ablaze with light, welcoming customers to come in and browse.

Mac had lived in Houston for a while, but he hadn't lasted long. Big cities were fun to go to for a few days, but his heart would always draw him back here. He liked the slower pace, the familiar faces and the views out his own windows. He liked knowing every inch of his surroundings and he enjoyed being in a place where everyone and their uncles and cousins made it their business to know yours.

"It's changed a lot from when we were kids," Andi mused, "but somehow it stays the same, too." She turned her head to look up at him. "You know what I mean? The heart of Royal is still small-town beautiful."

"Yeah, it is," he finally said, shifting his gaze to hers. Those gray eyes shone a little brighter with the gleam of lamplight reflected in their depths. It was enough to stop a man's heart if he wasn't careful. Which Mac generally was.

"You know," he said abruptly, "it's early yet. How about you come with me to the ranch? I can show you that mare you had to make all the travel arrangements for."

She bit down on her bottom lip as she considered it, and he tried not to watch. "I don't know. I've got a lot of things to do tomorrow and—"

"Being alone with me scare you a little?" he asked in a whispered hush.

Her gaze snapped to his. "I told you before, you don't scare me."

But she was nervous. He could see it. And that gave him the nudge to push her into coming out to his place. Maybe it wasn't a smart move, but right now he wasn't interested in being "smart." "Then there's no problem, is there?"

He'd delivered her a direct challenge, one she wouldn't be able to resist. He knew her as well as she did him, so Mac realized that she'd never say no. Because she wouldn't want him to think she was as uneasy as she obviously was.

Damn. His thoughts were starting to circle like a merry-go-round in a tornado. What was the woman doing to him?

"All right," she said, shaking him out of his own head, for which he was grateful. "But after you show me the mare, you take me home. Deal?"

He took her hand but instead of shaking it, lifted it to his mouth. Keeping his eyes on hers, he kissed her knuckles and saw the flare of heat flash across that cool, gray surface. Her skin was soft, smooth, and the scent of her pooled in his gut and began to burn. "We're making a lot of deals here lately, Andi."

She pulled her hand from his, and damned if he didn't miss the feel of her. "Just remember this one, okay? Horse, then home."

"Oh, I'll remember."

He opened the car door for her, then closed it firmly and smiled to himself. He didn't say how *long* it would be after she saw the horse that he would take her home. For a woman as organized and detail-oriented as she was, she'd really overlooked that particular loophole.

He smiled all the way to the ranch.

The twenty minute drive from town to the Double M ranch seemed to pass in seconds. Andi couldn't even enjoy the scenery they passed, with the moonlight wash-

ing over it all in a pale, cool light. She was way too tense
to appreciate the view, for heaven's sake.

The ride in Mac's Range Rover was smooth, and quiet
but for the Southern blues pumping from the stereo. She
hardly spoke because she had too many thoughts racing
through her mind. Mac didn't have much to say, she was
guessing by his smug smile, because he'd already gotten his way by getting her to go to his ranch with him.

Why was she going with him?

He had kissed her hand.

That one small, sexy action had pulled her in and
made it impossible for her to say no. Darn it, Mac was
being sweet and seductive and she felt herself weaken-
ing. She'd loved him for years, wanted him for years,
and now, for whatever reason, he'd turned his charm
onto her and she was slipping. Slipping down a slope
that was going to be so hard to climb back up.

At the edge of the McCallum ranch land, they passed
the office where she'd worked for six years. There were
low lights burning in the windows and the gravel parking lot was empty in the moonlight. A huge chunk of
her life had been spent there and a part of her was sorry
to see it go—the part that wanted to be with Mac, no
matter what.

Andi's stomach pitched and she shot him a careful
look from the corner of her eyes. He was smiling to himself and that only increased the anxiety already pumping through her. What was he thinking? Heck, what was
he planning?

How strange. She had believed she knew Mac better than anyone in the world. For years, she had antici-
pated his every professional need and rushed to meet it.
But the Mac who kissed her hand and gave her wicked

smiles over a shared bottle of wine while firelight shone in his eyes was a whole new ball game. She wasn't sure of her next move.

Frankly, she wasn't sure of much at the moment. But Amanda's words kept whispering through her mind. *Make time for a secret lover.* Is that what she was doing?

Heat zipped through her, head-to-toe, at the thought, leaving a lingering burn that sizzled somewhere in the middle. Going to bed with Mac was a bad idea and yet...

They turned off the main road and drove beneath the Double M gates, which swung open, then closed with a touch of a remote button. The land seemed to stretch out for miles, while the long drive to the ranch house was lined with oaks, their gnarled, twisting branches reaching for each other across the graveled drive. In full summer, this drive would be a shaded lane. Right now, there were still some bare branches that allowed moonlight to slip through and lie in silvered patches on the ground in front of them. At the end of the drive, the house waited.

A sprawling affair, it was two stories, built of stone and wood with wings that spread out from the center. More oaks stood sentinel at the corners of the house and the flower beds were a riot of color that even in the moonlit darkness looked cheerful and welcoming. The windows were lit, creating squares of gold across the front of the house, and the yard lights blinked on as Mac pulled up and parked.

Now what?

He hopped out of the car, came around to her side and opened the door, giving her a hand down. She appreciated it, since the heels she was currently teetering on weren't made for climbing. Or walking, when it came to it, which was why she winced when he took her hand and led her toward the stables.

"You know, I'm not really dressed for a barn visit—"

Mac glanced at her and one corner of his mouth tipped up. "It's okay. Next time you can dress up."

"What? Oh, for—"

He winked at her and kept walking.

That charm of his kept tugging at her and she was pretty sure he knew it. Andi huffed out a breath because clearly the man was not going to be dissuaded. Hurrying her steps to keep up with his much longer strides, she asked, "Is this a race?"

"Sorry," he said, and slowed down, never letting go of her hand. Not that she wanted him to. She liked the feel of his hard, calloused palm pressed close to hers.

That was the problem.

Every step they took crunched out into the country quiet. The soft breeze was still blowing and felt cool against her skin. Mac was a tall, solid presence at her side, and as they walked together in the moonlight, she had a hard time holding her all-too-eager heart back from taking a tumble to land at his feet.

"Soon enough, it'll be steaming hot here, but for now, it's a nice night for a walk."

She looked up at him. "It is. If you're wearing the right shoes."

"If you can't walk in them," he said, giving her heels a quick glance, "why wear them?"

"They're not for walking," she said. "They're for making my legs look great."

He took another look, a slow, lengthy one this time, then met her eyes with a smile. "Mission accomplished."

"Thanks." Her heart started that tumble again and she

steeled herself against giving in. She already loved the man. And the Mac she knew would run like a scalded cat if he knew it. In the past, any woman who'd started getting what he called the "white-fences gleam" in her eye had been set aside so fast their heads were probably still spinning.

If Andi didn't keep a grip on her feelings, she really would wind up lying alone in a dark room with nothing but her pain for company. So instead of concentrating on the man at her side, she looked around as they neared the stable.

The corral fences were painted white and stood out against the darkness like ghostly barricades. The stable itself was moon-washed and looked like a deeper shadow against the night. The barn farther off to the right was bigger, wider, to accommodate all of the equipment needed to keep a ranch of this size running. There were other outbuildings, too. A house for the ranch manager and his wife, a barracks of sorts where unmarried employees lived and a separate storage building where winter feed could be kept until it was needed.

Mac McCallum might be a wildly successful businessman, but at the core of him, Mac was a rancher. He would always love this land, this place, the horses and cattle he ran and the wide-open stretch of sky that seemed as if it went on forever. This ranch was in his blood, it was bred in his bones, and whether he acknowledged it or not, this place was the beating of his heart.

"You went quiet all of a sudden," he said. "A sure sign you're thinking too much again."

She laughed and shook her head. "Since when do you notice what I'm doing?"

"I always noticed, Andi," he said softly, and his voice

FREE Merchandise is 'in the Cards' for you!

Dear Reader,

We're giving away FREE MERCHANDISE!

Seriously, we'd like to reward you for reading this novel by giving you **FREE MERCHANDISE** worth over $20 retail. And no purchase is necessary!

It's easy! All you have to do is look inside for your Free Merchandise Voucher. Return the Voucher promptly…and we'll send you valuable Free Merchandise!

Thanks again for reading one of our novels—and enjoy your Free Merchandise with our compliments!

Pam Powers

Pam Powers

P.S. Look inside to see what Free Merchandise is **"in the cards"** for you!

W

e'd like to send you two free books like the one you are enjoying now. Your two books have a combined price of over $10 retail, but they are yours to keep absolutely FREE! We'll even send you 2 wonderful surprise gifts. You can't lose!

REMEMBER: Your Free Merchandise, consisting of **2 Free Books** and **2 Free Gifts**, is worth over $20 retail! No purchase is necessary, so please send for your Free Merchandise today.

FREE MERCHANDISE VOUCHER

❑ Please send my Free Merchandise, consisting of
2 Free Books and **2 Free Mystery Gifts**.
I understand that I am under no obligation to buy
anything, as explained on the back of this card.

225/326 HDL GKAY

Please Print

FIRST NAME

LAST NAME

ADDRESS

APT.#   CITY

STATE/PROV.   ZIP/POSTAL CODE

Offer limited to one per household and not applicable to series that subscriber is currently receiving.
Your Privacy—The Reader Service is committed to protecting your privacy. Our Privacy Policy is available online at www.ReaderService.com or upon request from the Reader Service. We make a portion of our mailing list available to reputable third parties that offer products we believe may interest you. If you prefer that we not exchange your name with third parties, or if you wish to clarify or modify your communication preferences, please visit us at www.ReaderService.com/consumerschoice or write to us at Reader Service Preference Service, P.O. Box 9062, Buffalo, NY 14240-9062. Include your complete name and address.

NO PURCHASE NECESSARY!

HD-516-FMH16

▼ If offer card is missing write to: Reader Service, P.O. Box 1867, Buffalo, NY 14240-1867 or visit www.ReaderService.com ▼

BUSINESS REPLY MAIL
FIRST-CLASS MAIL   PERMIT NO. 717   BUFFALO, NY

POSTAGE WILL BE PAID BY ADDRESSEE

READER SERVICE
PO BOX 1867
BUFFALO NY 14240-9952

NO POSTAGE
NECESSARY
IF MAILED
IN THE
UNITED STATES

slipped inside her to caress every last nerve ending. "Though I'll admit, I just took you for granted before."

"Really?"

He glanced at her and smiled. "Don't be so surprised. Even I can grow some."

How was she supposed to fall *out* of love with a man who could say something like that?

"I figured," he continued, "that you'd always be there when I needed you. In my own defense, though, you're the one who caused me to believe it."

Wryly, she shook her head and smiled. "So it's my fault."

"Absolutely."

She laughed again. "Well, then, I'm so very sorry."

"Don't be," he said and drew them to a stop. Hands on her arms, he turned her to face him. "I wouldn't change a damn thing, except for the idea of you quitting."

"It's not an idea. It's fact. You can't change it, Mac. It already happened."

"Don't count me out just yet," he warned, one corner of his mouth lifting into that half smile that did amazing things to the pit of her stomach.

It was a scene built for romance. If she wasn't living it, Andi would have thought it was like being in the pages of a romance novel. Moonlight, soft breezes, stars glittering overhead and a tall, gorgeous man looking down at her as if she were the center of the universe.

Just for a moment, for the length of a single heartbeat, Andi wished it were true. Wished she and Mac were a couple. That they were here on *their* home ranch, taking a walk in the moonlight before going upstairs together.

Then the moment passed and reality came crashing

back down on her. "Um, you going to show me that mare?"

"You bet," he said, then in one smooth move bent down, scooped one arm under her legs and swung her up against him.

So surprised she could hardly speak, Andi just gaped at him. Whether he knew it or not, he was really filling in the blanks on her romantic fantasy.

"Mac!" She pushed ineffectually at his chest and wasn't surprised at all when she didn't make a dent. "What are you doing?"

"Look there," he said, jerking his head to a spot just ahead of them.

She did, and saw a mud puddle that stretched from the stable fence to nearly the back of the ranch house. "Oh."

"That's right." He looked down at her. "Those pretty shoes of yours would never make it through the mud. A shame to ruin them."

"Or," she said, squirming a little in his hard, tight grasp, "I just won't go see the horse tonight. Put me down."

"Nope, we had a deal. I'll carry you to the stable." He started walking and then added, "Guess I just have to rescue you again. How many does that make now?" he wondered aloud. "Are you keeping count?"

"This isn't a rescue," she said, not completely able to hide the exasperated laughter bubbling from her throat as she wrapped her arms around his neck. "This is a kidnapping."

"Is that right?" He shrugged and hefted her just a little higher in his arms. "Well, it's my first."

"Congratulations."

"Thanks." He looked at her again. "I'm having a hell of a good time."

"Strangely enough," she said wistfully, "so am I."

He stopped, stared down into her eyes. "Good to know."

A couple of humming, electrical seconds passed while they stared at each other and the soft, early summer breeze wrapped itself around them. She was in so much trouble, Andi told herself.

Finally, he went on, carrying her across the muddy water and into the stable, where the scents of fresh hay and horses greeted them. It was quiet but for the occasional stamp of a hoof against the floor. Slowly, Mac set her on her feet, but caught her hand in his and held tight.

"Come on," he said, "I'll show you the mare."

They walked the length of the freshly swept aisle between stalls and as they passed horses poked their heads out as if to say hello. Mac had a moment with each of them, stroking noses, murmuring soft words to the animals until Andi was half convinced they were actually communicating.

At the last stall, he stopped and smiled at a gray horse with a blond mane as the animal reached out her nose toward him. "Andi, this is Moonlight."

"She's beautiful." She stroked the horse's neck and jaw, loving the soft, sturdy feel of the friendly mare.

"Yeah," Mac said, shifting his gaze from the mare to her. "She is. And this pretty girl's going to produce some beautiful children over the next few years."

"Who's the proud father-to-be?"

"Ah," he said, giving the mare one last pat before turning and pointing to a stall twice as big as the other animals had. "That would be Apollo."

The stallion was a dark, sleek brown with a black mane and tail, and he held his head high and aloof as if he knew just how important he was.

"He looks as if he thinks of himself as a god, so, appropriate name," Andi said.

"For a stallion, he's got a great temperament, too." They walked closer and the big horse shook his head and snorted.

"Yeah, I can see he's really friendly," Andi said, laughing nervously.

"He just doesn't like being tied down. He'd rather be out in the corral kicking up his heels than shut down for the night."

"So he's definitely male."

One eyebrow lifted. "Is that a slur against my gender?"

"Not a slur. An observation," she said, walking back up the aisle, pausing now and again to say hello to one of the horses or to stroke or pat.

"Based on your vast experience?" he teased from just a step behind her.

She looked over her shoulder at him. "I've known a few who've taken off for the hills as soon as anything remotely serious pops up. Take you, for example."

"Me?" He slapped one hand to his chest as if deeply wounded.

She laughed again, enjoying herself in the quiet, dimly lit stable. "Please. How many times have I purchased the see-you-later-thanks-for-the-memories bracelets?"

He winced and that only made her laugh harder. "Admit it, Mac. It's not only when you get bored with a woman that you move on. It's also when she starts getting stars in her eyes over you. Much like your stallion over there, you prefer running free. The only real commitment you've ever made was to the business."

"Maybe," he said, taking her arm and pulling her around to face him, "it's because I haven't met the right woman yet."

"Not for lack of trying," she said wryly.

He grinned and shrugged that off. "I'm no quitter."

He slid his hands up her arms to cup her face between his work-roughened palms. His thumbs stroked her cheekbones as his gaze met hers and held, warming the longer he looked at her. "You're confusing me, Andi," he said so softly she wasn't sure she'd heard him correctly.

Andi felt that rush of heat she'd come to expect from his touch, then her breath caught when the heat exploded into an inferno as he leaned down, bringing his mouth just inches from hers. If she had a single working brain cell, she would move back, keep a distance between them. A kiss from Mac was going to lead to places she really shouldn't consider going.

But she couldn't think. What woman could under the same circumstances? Her heartbeat sounded like a bass drum in her own ears. Breathe, she reminded herself. *Breathe.*

He smiled, a slow, slight curve of his mouth. "What's the matter, Andi? Feeling a little nervous after all?"

"No." *Liar.* Nerves, yes. Excitement, oh yes. Worry? She should be worried. Instead there was a tiny, faint voice crying out for caution, trying to be heard over the clamor of need screaming in her head.

She licked her lips and watched his eyes flare at the motion.

"Seduction in a stable, Mac?"

"The horses won't mind," he assured her.

"Maybe not," she whispered, her gaze dropping briefly to his mouth before meeting his again. "But I should."

His hands stilled as he stared into her eyes. "Do you?"

"No."

"Thank God."

She leaned into him and he moved quickly, laying his mouth over hers. Andi thought she heard herself groan, but that was the last thought she had. It was impossible to think when so many sensations were awakening, demanding to be relished, explored.

He pulled her tight against him, his arms coming around her like a vise, squeezing as though he thought she might try to escape his hold. But that was the last thing Andi wanted. This was probably a mistake and no doubt she'd come to regret it at some point, but at the moment, all she could think was *yes*. *Touch me. Hold me. Be with me.*

For six years, she'd loved him. For six years, she'd hidden everything she felt. Now finally, if only for this one night, she would be with the man she loved. Know what it was like to hold his body close to hers. To take him inside. And she wouldn't give up that chance for any amount of logic and reason.

He drew his head back and looked down at her, eyes wide, flashing with emotions that changed too quickly for her to read. But maybe that was for the best.

"Man," he whispered. "Should have done that a long time ago."

"Now is good, too," she said, though her voice sounded breathy and so unlike her she hardly recognized it. Her whole body was humming with impatience, with need. She was practically vibrating with the tension coiled tight in the pit of her stomach.

"Now is *great*," he amended, then swept her up into his arms again.

"What are you doing?"

"Just another rescue," he said, and headed out of the stable. But instead of going toward his car, Mac made a right turn and started for the ranch house. "This time, though," he told her, "I'm saving us both."

Seven

Andi held on, then leaned up and kissed the side of his neck. Her decision was made. There would be no turning back now. Tonight, she would make memories that years from now she'd relive and remember. "Hurry."

A low, throaty growl rolled from his throat, but he did exactly as she ordered, his long legs eating up the distance to the house in a few minutes. Overhead, the sky was black with a wide sweep of stars impossible to see unless you were outside a city, away from the lights. A nearly full moon glowed against the blackness and sent that wash of light over everything like a blessing. The warm June wind wrapped itself around them and swept them on toward the lamplit house ahead of them.

He opened the door, stepped through and kicked it shut behind him. The kitchen lay empty and still in the glow of a stove light, but Mac didn't stop to admire the elegantly remodeled space.

Andi barely had a chance to admire it, even if she'd been interested, before he was across the room and striding down a long hallway. They passed a dining room, Mac's study and the great room at the front of the house before he came to the wide oak staircase, where he suddenly stopped.

Surprised, Andi tore her gaze away from the massive iron and wood chandelier hanging from the cathedral ceiling over the foyer to look into his eyes. A view she preferred.

"What is it? What's wrong?" Her heart galloped in her chest as his hands held her in a proprietary grasp.

Keeping her pressed tightly against him, Mac said, "Nothing's wrong as far as I'm concerned. I'm just checking one last time."

She smiled and trailed the tips of her fingers along his jaw and throat. He shivered, then sucked in a gulp of air like a drowning man tasting hope.

She smiled, loving his response. And she knew exactly what he was doing now. Mac being Mac, he was giving her one last chance to change her mind about what was about to happen. He was charming, gorgeous and had a sense of honor that not enough men these days possessed. How could she resist him?

But still she asked innocently, "Checking what?"

"God help me," Mac said, letting his head fall back helplessly. "Yes or no, Andi. Don't make me beg."

"It's a big step," she teased. "I just don't know…"

He narrowed his eyes on her and gave her a hard squeeze. "Woman, you're treading on thin ice here."

She smiled and asked, "How fast can you take these stairs?"

His grin flashed bright. "We're about to find out."

Probably silly, Andi thought as her heart raced, to feel such a wild rush of pleasure at the man she loved holding her close and sprinting up a staircase.

She'd been in the house before, to see Vi when she'd lived in the west wing. But Andi now caught glimpses of Mac's side of the house when he made a sharp right at the top of the stairs. She couldn't have been less interested in the decor, but noted the Western paintings on the cream-colored walls as he passed. She saw the heavy, dark beams on the ceiling and heard every muffled boot step on the carpet runner along the hall. Then he turned into his bedroom and Andi focused only on him.

He swung her to her feet, but didn't let her go. Instead, he cradled her close to his chest, lowered his head to hers and kissed her breathless.

There was no slow slide into delight here; this was like a fall on a roller coaster. A whoosh of sensation that rushed through the blood and then gave you just enough time to breathe before starting all over again.

His hands, those big, strong hands, were everywhere at once—sliding up and down her spine, around to cup her breasts and then up to touch her face, fingers spearing through her hair, tipping her head first one way then the other as he deepened a kiss that was already searing her soul.

"I've been wanting my hands on you," he murmured when he tore his mouth from hers.

"I've been wanting that, too." *For so long.*

"Glad to hear it," he said, giving her the wicked half smile that never failed to send jolts of anticipation rocketing through her. And now, that sensation was going to have a payoff. At last.

He turned her around, her back to his front, and

tugged her zipper down slowly. She sighed, air sliding from her lungs on a half moan at the touch of his fingers against her back.

The bed in front of her was huge. Like an adult playground, with a midnight-blue duvet and a dozen pillows propped at the headboard. Across the room, there were French doors that led out onto the second-story balcony and a door on the right of the room that no doubt led to a bathroom suite. A cold hearth stood on one side of the room and there were two matching leather comfy chairs in front of it.

She wasn't feeling comfy at the moment, though; she was on edge, every nerve in her body tingling with expectation. Mac slid the shoulder straps of her dress down her arms and followed the motion with his mouth. Lips, teeth, tongue trailed over her skin and made her shiver. She couldn't believe this was happening. After six long years of loving, she was finally *being* loved by the man she'd thought she could never have.

And even if this was only one night, it was one she would always remember. She would etch it into her memory so she could replay it over and over again. Relish every touch, every breath, every sigh—and regret that it hadn't lasted longer than one night.

"I wanted slow and seductive," he admitted as he turned her to face him and watched as the bodice of her dress dropped to her waist, displaying a strapless black lace bra. His eyes went wide and hot as he lifted his gaze to hers. "But I find I'm too hungry for you to take my time."

"Me, too, Mac." She'd wanted for so long, needed so much; this was no time for lazy caresses and tenderness.

This was a rush to fulfillment. To ease the aches they both felt. And she was ready.

Andi reached for the buttons on his shirt even as he shrugged off his jacket and let it fall. When the shirt lay open, she splayed her hands on his hard, muscled chest and felt his heart pound in time with her own. His eyes caught hers and locked, passion glittering bright and sharp in those green depths. He kissed her again, long and deep, eliciting another groan from her as he tumbled her back onto the bed and followed her down. He tore his own shirt off, then came back to her, sliding her dress down her hips and taking her black lace panties with it. He pushed them off and onto the floor.

The duvet felt silky and cool against her back, adding contrasting layers to the sizzling warmth pumping through her. Andi unhooked her bra and watched his eyes as her breasts were bared to him. Heat flashed in his gaze just before he lowered his head to take, first, one rigid nipple, then the other into his mouth. His tongue lapped at her, his lips and teeth tugged and suckled at her, and in seconds, Andi was writhing beneath him, moving with the need erupting like lava in her blood. She held his head to her and watched him, and her mind spun out into sparkle-splashed darkness. There was nothing in the world but the two of them. This moment. This bed. This...wonder.

Then he moved up her body and took her mouth again, their tongues tangling together in a frenzied dance of passion that fed the fires already burning inside them both.

His right hand swept down her length and into the heat of her. She was wound so tight, had waited so long, that that first intimate touch was enough to make her shatter in tiny, helpless waves of pleasure that flickered and shone like lit sparklers just beneath her skin. "Mac…"

"Just getting started, darlin'," he promised, and delved deep, his fingers stroking, caressing already sensitive skin until she lifted her hips into his hand, hoping to ease the sudden burst of need that continued to build.

"I can't do this again so soon." Proud of herself for getting the words out, she clutched at his shoulders and held on as her body did things she hadn't expected it could.

Always before, sex had been a soft, almost sweet release of tension. A gentle ripple that drifted through her body on a tender sigh of completion.

This was different. That soft ripple had already washed away in a rising tide of fresh need that swamped everything that had come before.

He kissed her mouth, her shoulders, her breasts; he touched her deeply, intimately, and watched her every reaction. She gave him everything she had. She showed him everything she felt. Andi held nothing back because she'd waited too long to feel it all.

His touch was fire. His eyes were magic. She felt her own body jumping out of her control and she let it go.

Another climax hit her, stronger than the last, and she cried out his name as her body trembled and shook beneath his hands. But he wasn't finished, she realized as she lay there, struggling for air, trying to make her mind clear enough to appreciate just where she was.

She opened her eyes and saw him slide off the bed, strip off the rest of his clothes. Her eyes went wide as she looked at his amazing body, so lean and strong and sculpted. And for tonight at least…hers.

He joined her on the bed again, this time covering her

body with his, sliding up the length of her. Andi's hands and nails scraped up and down his back. Her legs parted, lifted, welcoming him to her, and when he entered her, she gasped and arched at the swift invasion. He felt so good. So right. So big. He filled her until it seemed as though they'd joined on much more than a physical level.

In this moment, they were one unit, and as she moved with him, she stared up into his eyes and lost herself in the wild gleam she saw there. He plunged into her heat, and unbelievably, she responded by tightening into another fiercer ball of tension deep inside. She felt the now familiar buildup and knew that this time, when he pushed her over the edge, it would be shattering. She couldn't wait.

So when he pulled away from her, Andi nearly whimpered with the boiling need clawing at her. But he paused only long enough to dig into the bedside table drawer and grab a condom.

"Damn," he said, glancing at her. "I was so caught up in you I almost forgot protection."

"You're not alone in that. I can't believe it, but I wasn't thinking—"

"Who needs to think?" he asked, and in a second he was back, buried inside her, and the two of them raced toward the finish line.

She held him, hooked her legs around his waist even as he reached under her with one hand and lifted her hips. Andi struggled to breathe, gave up any attempt to hang on to sanity and threw herself into the moment with an abandon she'd never experienced before.

Here was the difference, she thought wildly, between sparklers and skyrockets. Pleasure slammed into her with a crash, making it hard to breathe and harder to care. As the first incredible eruptions exploded inside her, she cupped his face between her hands and looked deeply into the green of his eyes as she jumped into the void.

She was still holding him when his eyes glazed over, his hips pumped against her and he tumbled into the same starlit darkness with her.

Minutes, hours, heck, maybe *weeks* later, Andi's brain started working again. She simply lay there, completely spent. She loved the feel of Mac lying on top of her and would have been perfectly content to stay in just that position from now until whenever. But even as that thought slipped through her mind, he was rolling to one side of her. He kept one arm wrapped around her, though, and pulled her in close, nestling her head on his chest. She heard the frantic pounding of his heart and knew her own was racing, as well.

God, she'd never been through anything like that before. Every other sexual experience she'd had in her life paled alongside what she'd just lived through. The man was…gifted.

"That was," he whispered into the darkness, "well, I don't think I can find a word for it."

"Yeah," she agreed. "Me, either."

He rolled her over onto her back and levered himself up until he was looking down into her eyes. "Can't believe it took us six years to do that."

"It was worth the wait," she told him.

"And then some," he agreed, pushing her hair off her shoulder, dipping his head to kiss that warm curve at the base of her throat.

Andi shivered again. Oh, she was in so much trouble. When she'd first decided that going to bed with Mac was a good idea, there'd been a small part of her convinced that if she did, it might help her get over him. Get past the feelings she had for him so she could move on with her own life. Instead, she was in even deeper trouble than she had been before.

He hadn't made love only to her body, but to her heart, too. Love welled up and spilled over. She wasn't going to get over him. Ever. And that was a thought designed for misery. Because he didn't love her back. And there was just no lonelier feeling in the world than loving someone who didn't love you.

He lifted his head, smiled down at her and said, "Hope you're up for a repeat performance, because I don't think I'm done with you yet."

She loved hearing that, and there was nothing she'd like more. The idea of staying right there in that big bed with Mac was more appealing than she could admit. She wanted to watch the sunrise with him. Wanted to be here again in the evening and spend her nights wrapped around him.

But none of that was going to happen.

Andi had already indulged herself; now it was time to start protecting herself. For her own good.

"That's probably not a good idea," she said.

"Why the hell not?" he demanded, tightening his hold on her as if she might try to get out of bed.

Which she really should.

"Because this—between us—it's not going anywhere, Mac, so what's the point?"

He laughed. "You can ask me that after what we just shared? Andi, that was incredible."

"It was," she said, starting to feel the chill of the room on her skin. "And now we're done."

"Don't have to be," he told her, bending down to kiss her once, twice, just a brush of her lips with his. "Andi, this just proves what I've been saying all along. We make a great team."

"A team?" The chill she felt deepened as she waited for him to continue.

"Yeah." Idly, he ran one hand over her skin until he finally cupped one of her breasts. As he talked, his fingertips caressed her.

A new wash of heat swept over her, but was lost in the chill when he continued.

"We're a team, Andi. At the office. Clearly, in bed." He dropped his head, kissed her briefly, then looked at her, satisfaction shining in his eyes. "You've got to come back to work now. Can't you see what a mistake it would be to walk away from everything we have together?"

Okay. The chill was now icy. Her heart was full of love and all he could think about was using sex to get her back to the office? She brushed his hand aside and scooted back from him. Her own nudity didn't bother her; she was much too consumed by a temper that bubbled and frothed in the pit of her stomach to worry about being naked.

She knew he'd felt what she had when they came together. He couldn't have been immune to the incredible sense of "rightness" that had lit up between them. Could he? Could he have experienced just what she had and explain it all away as *teamwork*?

Sad, that's what it was. Just sad. But anger was better than sorrow, so she gave herself over to it.

"Seriously?" she asked, shaking her hair back from her face. "You think promising me more sex will keep me as your assistant?"

"Why not?" He grinned again, clearly not picking up on the ice in her tone. "Honey, we just made the world tremble. I don't know about you, but I've never experienced anything even remotely like it before. Why the hell wouldn't we do that again? As often as possible?"

He couldn't see why and she couldn't tell him. So they were at an impasse. One that wasn't going to be maneuvered around. Before she could say anything, he started talking again, clearly enthused with his idea.

"As long as no one at the office knows what's going on between us, we can go on being lovers and work together just like we did before."

He reached for her, but she shook her head. "Just like before."

"Yeah." His smile slipped a little as if he were beginning to pick up on the fact that she wasn't all that enthused with his "plan." But still, he kept going. "We work together, each have our own homes and we share amazing sex."

"So we're boss and assistant at the office and bed buddies once that door's closed."

He frowned. "Bed buddies seems a little—"

"Accurate?"

"Okay, something's bothering you."

She laughed shortly and the sound of it scraped across her throat. "Yeah. Something."

God, she was an idiot. Yes, she had the memory of this night to cling to, but now, she'd also have the memory of this conversation to color it. How could he be so smart and so stupid all at once? And how could she have walked right into this situation, a smile on her face and eagerness in her heart?

"It's the best of all possible worlds, Andi," he said, voice deep, low. "What could be better?"

So many things, she thought. Love. Commitment. Marriage. Family. The offer he'd just made her paled in comparison. She couldn't say any of that, of course. For him, love had never entered the picture and damned if she'd shove it through the door now.

"No." Shaking her head, she scooted off the bed and grabbed her dress off the floor.

"No?" he echoed, sitting up to stare at her. "That's all you've got to say? Just...no?"

"Just no." Stepping into the dress, she pulled it up, then fought with the zipper. Andi was so done. She needed to get out of there. Fast. Before she said too much of what she was thinking. Problem? She didn't have her car. She'd be trapped in his all the way back to town. Nearly groaning in frustration now, she tugged again at the *stupid* zipper, which remained stuck.

Still, psychologically, she felt much more able to have a fight if she at least wasn't naked.

"Why no, Andi?" He came off the bed, too, and went to grab her shoulders before she slipped away. His eyes fired. "Is there someone else? Some guy I don't know about? Is that what this is?"

She looked at him in disbelief. "Are you kidding? *When* could I possibly have found a guy, Mac?" She whipped her hair behind her shoulders, tugged at the damned zipper again and knew she'd snagged it in the fabric. Letting her arms fall to her sides, she glared at him as if even the zipper was his fault. "Until several days ago I was pretty much an indentured servant. I had no life outside that office."

"Servant?" His eyes flashed and this time it was anger

pumping from him, not sexual energy. "A damn well-paid servant if you're asking me."

"I'm not," she countered.

"Well, you should." He shoved one hand through his hair and gritted his teeth.

"Sure, I made a great salary—and had zero chance to spend any of it." Andi met his anger with her own and stood her ground, just as she always had. "How do you think I can afford to quit? I've got everything you ever paid me sitting in a bank account."

"That's great." He threw his hands up and let them fall again. "So I'm *paying* you to leave me."

"In a nutshell." She looked around wildly, searching for her shoes. He'd carried her in here, and right now that little romantic moment felt light-years away. Had she kicked them off? Had he pulled them off? Did it matter?

"There!" She spotted one of her heels under a chair near the fireplace. Surely the other one would be close.

"What're you doing?"

"It should be obvious." She picked up one shoe and continued the search for the other. "I'm getting dressed. I need to go home."

"You can't leave in the middle of a fight."

She saw the other shoe and snatched it. "Watch me."

"How?"

God, she was so done. Andi couldn't believe that what had started out as an amazing evening had devolved into a battle. And what was she fighting for? He didn't want to be won. He wanted his assistant back—with fringe benefits. How humiliating was that?

"How what?" She pulled her shoes on, straightened up and glanced at Mac.

"How are you going to leave?" He was still blissfully

naked and it was a struggle to keep her hormones from jumping up and down just from looking at him. His arms were folded across his chest, his green eyes were narrowed. "It's a hell of a long hike from the ranch to town. Especially in those heels."

Here was the problem she'd noted earlier. "Damn it, you have to drive me."

"When we're done talking," Mac said.

"Oh," Andi told him, nodding, "trust me, we're done."

"You can't tell me that what just happened between us didn't change something."

"It changed *everything*," she said, wishing she'd suddenly sprout wings so she could just jump off his balcony and get herself home. Now. "That's the point."

"And my point is, that change doesn't have to be a bad one."

If he only knew. "Mac…"

He pulled her in close and though she was still pretty angry, she didn't fight him on it. Tipping her head back, she looked into his eyes and wished things were different. Wished she didn't love him so damn much. Wished he felt even a touch of what she felt.

"Don't say no so fast, Andi," he whispered, tucking a stray lock of her hair behind her ear. She shivered at the gentle touch and knew that something inside her was melting in spite of everything. What kind of fool did that make her?

"Wait," he said. "See." He winked. "I've still got most of the two weeks I took off left to help you set up your house. Get it in order. Let's see where we are at the end of it. Okay?"

At the end of the two weeks, they would be in the same damn place, only she'd be even more twisted up and torn over it. There was no way to win in this particular battle. When it was over they would both lose something, and she couldn't prevent that, even if it ended tonight.

So did she take the rest of those two weeks, torment herself with dreams that had no basis in reality? Or did she end it now, while she was cold and empty and sad?

"Give us the time, Andi," he urged, and caressed her cheek with the backs of his fingers. "Let's find out together where we are at the end of it."

"I know where we'll be," she said, shaking her head.

"You can't, because I don't." His gaze moved over her face and Andi felt it as she would have a touch.

"Give it a chance," he said. "Don't end it now."

Fool, she told herself. *Don't be an idiot*, her brain warned. *Step back now and make it a clean break*, her heart shouted.

But she looked up into his eyes and didn't listen to any of it.

"Okay."

Eight

Mac didn't have his phone on him and realized that it was the first time in years he'd been completely disconnected from the rest of the world. He owed Andi for that. For making him see just how attached he'd gotten to the damn thing. Now, he could go hours without even thinking about his phone, and wasn't that amazing?

As thoughts of Andi rose up in his mind, though, he forgot about his phone and wondered what she was doing. Where she was. He hadn't been able to stop thinking about her since he dropped her off at her place the night before. Who could blame him? He never would have guessed at the woman behind the cool, professional demeanor. She'd hidden that from him so well, it had to make him wonder what other secrets she had. For the first time in his life, he wanted to know more about a woman, not less. And for the first time in his life, the woman wasn't interested.

"How the hell can she not be?" he muttered, scrawling his signature across the bottom of a contract. He tossed the papers to one side and reached for the next stack.

Last night with Andi had been a revelation. He'd been with his share of women over the years, but nothing he'd ever experienced had come close to what had happened between them. Being locked inside her body had taken him higher than ever before. Her every breath, every sigh had somehow drifted within him, taking root and blossoming so richly he'd hardly been able to breathe. Touching her had awakened a tenderness in him he hadn't been aware of. Need hadn't been satisfied. If anything, it had grown, until now he felt as if he were choking with it.

He'd wanted her to stay with him last night. Another first. He didn't usually take women to his home, and on the rare occasions he had, he'd hustled them back out again as quickly as possible. But this time, it had been Andi who'd drawn a line in the sand.

Mac could admit, at least to himself, that when she'd jumped out of bed with the idea of closing things off between them, he'd felt—not panic, he assured himself— more like a sense of being rattled. He'd thought that after what they'd shared, she'd turn cuddly and, damn it, *agreeable*. Instead, she'd refused to see reason and had almost cut him off.

That had never happened before.

He didn't like it.

Pausing in his work, he tightened his grip on the sterling silver pen and stared blindly at the wall opposite, not seeing his office but the woman currently driving him around the bend.

When he dropped her off at her place, they'd agreed

to take the next day apart, to catch up on things that had to be done—but more than that, they'd both needed some time to come to grips with what had happened between them. So Mac was here, signing off on the contracts his lawyers had approved and Andi was…where?

Damn it.

He grabbed his desk phone, punched in a number and waited while it rang. When a familiar voice answered, Mac said, "Rafe. You open for lunch today?"

Mac needed to talk to another guy. A man would understand. Women were just too damned confusing.

"Yes," Rafe said. "I'm free. Is there something wrong?"

"Damned if I know," Mac muttered. "I was sort of hoping you could help me figure that out."

"Well, now I wouldn't miss lunch for anything. The diner then? About one?"

"That'll work." Mac hung up and got back to the business at hand.

Thoughts of Andi nibbled at his mind, of course. The office seemed empty without the sound of her voice or the click of her sensible black pumps on the floor. He kept expecting her to give her perfunctory knock before throwing his door open to tell him where he needed to be.

Instead, he had a neatly typed-up schedule from Laura—with no notations like *be on time* written in red ink in the margins. His office was running along and he had to admit they seemed to be managing without him fairly well.

Tim would be back next week and, meanwhile, phone calls between Laura and him were keeping everything going while Mac was gone. He didn't know how he felt about that, to be honest.

Finished signing the stack of papers, he tossed his pen

onto the desk and leaned back in his leather chair. He swiveled to look out a window at the spread of McCallum land and told himself that he should be pleased. Work was getting done. Clients were happy. Papers were being filed. It seemed his company didn't need his 24/7 dedication after all. Exactly what Andi had been trying to tell him.

So had he just been wasting his life locked away here in this building? He'd devoted himself to his job, to the exclusion of everything else only to find that the business ran just fine without him. What the hell did that say?

To him, it said that he couldn't sit here anymore. Why the hell did he agree to take this time away from Andi when all he really wanted was to be with her?

Disgusted with his own company, Mac picked up the contracts and carried them out to the main office. Dumping them all on Laura's desk, he said, "These are ready to go out."

"I'll take care of it right away," she assured him.

Mac noticed she still looked wary of him, so he made the effort to drop the brusqueness from his tone. "You're doing a great job, Laura. It's appreciated."

Surprised, she blinked up at him and a shy smile curved her mouth. "Thanks, Mr. McCallum."

He nodded. "Call me Mac. And if you've got any questions, you give Tim a call, all right?"

"I will." As he pushed open the door, he heard her call out, "Have a good day, Mac."

Not much chance of that.

"Thanks for coming out with me today, Violet."

"Are you kidding?" Vi held up several bags. "I love shopping here."

The Courtyard was just a few miles west of downtown Royal. It had begun as a ranch, then was taken over and renovated to become a bustling collection of eclectic shops. There were antiques, yarn and fabric stores, an artisan cheese maker and most Saturday mornings there was a farmer's market. You could get all the local produce you wanted, along with fresh flowers, not to mention the food stands that popped up to feed the hungry shoppers.

Since it was a long drive from Royal into the big city, having the Courtyard here was a real bonus to everyone for miles around. But as popular a spot as it was, Andi hadn't had the chance to really explore it as much as she'd wanted to. Working nonstop for Mac had kept her from doing a lot of things. But how could she regret time spent with him now that it was over?

"Anything in particular you're looking for?"

"Well, I do have a house to finally furnish," Andi said wistfully.

"Fun," Vi said. "And I'd like to stop in at the soap makers, then pop into Priceless. Raina's holding an antique rocking chair for me."

Raina Patterson Dane ran the antiques store, but she'd made it so much more by also offering craft classes in the back. Still, the furniture and wild mix of decor items had made Priceless *the* place to find different kinds of things for your house. Plus her new husband, Nolan, was opening his law office in the loft space above Priceless, so it really was a family affair.

"Sure," Andi said, turning to head over there. "I wanted to look there for the furniture, anyway."

"Good idea," Vi said as they walked side by side. "Priceless has so many nice things, I always need a truck to haul it all home when I'm finished in there. I swear every time I tell Rafe I'm going shopping, I can almost hear him thinking, *Please, not Priceless*."

Andi didn't believe her for a minute. Vi's husband was so in love with her, he supported everything she said or did. "Rafe wants you happy."

"He really does," Vi said, and ran one hand over her belly. "And I am. Completely. God, I didn't think I'd ever get to this place, you know? Things were so muddled with Rafe for a while, I was afraid we were going to lose what we'd found together."

Andi knew just how she felt. The only difference between them was that Andi *knew* she was going to lose what was most important to her. It was just a matter of time. Less than two weeks now, to be exact.

"I'm really glad," she finally said, trying to keep that twinge of envy she felt to herself.

"Oh man." Vi came to an abrupt stop and stared at Andi. "I'm so insensitive, I should be horsewhipped. There's something wrong, isn't there? That's why the spontaneous shopping invitation today. What happened?" Her shoulders slumped and she winced. "Did Mac do something? Should I have *him* horsewhipped?"

"Thanks for the offer." Andi laughed and reached out to hug her friend. "But no, you don't have to go after your brother. I swear, Vi, I don't know what I'd do without you and Jolene."

"Well, you don't have to know, do you?" She frowned. "Speaking of Jolene, why isn't she with us on this expedition?"

Andi had called her sister first thing that morning and told her everything—about her amazing night with Mac and then how it had ended not in joy, but with a whimper. Naturally Jolene had been thrilled, then sad, then furious on her behalf. How did people live without a sister to bitch to? Since Jolene hadn't been able to join Andi and Vi today, she'd made Andi give a solemn promise to come by later with more information. "She couldn't come. Jacob had a ball game."

"That's so nice." Vi's eyes went misty as she rubbed her belly again. "We'll have ball games, too, won't we, baby?"

"What if it's a girl?"

"Well, we'll find out soon," Vi reminded her, "And if it is a girl, I'll have to say that I was the starting shortstop on my Little League team."

"I stand corrected."

"Okay, but can we do it sitting down for a minute?" Vi pointed to several cushioned iron tables and chairs positioned close to the bakery. "Maybe get a scone and some tea?"

"Great idea." Once Andi had Vi sitting down comfortably, she said, "You stay here and watch our bags. I'll get the food and drinks."

It wasn't long before Andi was carrying a tray with two iced teas and two blueberry scones back to the table. The minute she set it down, Vi snatched at a scone. "Sorry I'm so greedy, but the baby's hungry all the time."

Wistful, Andi sighed a little. She had nieces and a nephew she loved. She could watch her best friend hurrying toward motherhood. But the chances of Andi ever having a child of her own were slim to none, since the only man she wanted to father her children couldn't be less interested.

"Now that I'm sitting down—thank you for that—and

baby's getting a scone…tell me, what's got that puckered-up look on your face?"

"My what?"

"You know." Vi wrinkled her brow and pursed her lips.

"Oh fine," Andi muttered and deliberately evened out her features.

"It's Mac, isn't it?" Vi set down the scone and took a sip of tea. "No one can wrinkle a woman's forehead like my brother."

"Sad, but true." Andi took a quick look around to make sure no one was close enough to overhear. But there were only a few other people taking a break and they were seated a couple of tables over.

Shoppers wandered, a toddler whined for a toy and a busy mom pushed a stroller at a fast trot while she kept a tight grip on a five-year-old. Everything was so ordinary. So normal. But Andi's world had been knocked completely out of whack.

She looked at Vi. "I slept with him."

"Mac?" Her friend's eyes popped wide and her mouth dropped open. "You slept with my brother?"

Hunching her shoulders a little, Andi whispered, "Could you maybe not shout it loud enough to spread it through town like a brushfire?"

"Sorry, sorry." Vi winced and leaned in over the table. "This is so great, Andi. I mean really. I've hoped and hoped you two would get together and finally it's happened. Tell me everything. Well, not everything, but you know. When? Why? No, never mind why. I know why, you're nuts about him, which could just make you literally nuts, but never mind. When?"

"Last night and yes, I probably am nuts." She was

glad that Vi was so happy about the situation. Andi only wished she could be. Breaking off a tiny piece of her scone, she nibbled at it. "I don't know what I was thinking."

"If it's like what happened with Rafe and I, you weren't thinking at all." Vi sat back, took another bite of her scone. "I don't think you're *supposed* to think about something that big. You're supposed to *feel* it."

Oh, there had been lots of feeling. Sadly, it had been all on her side. "Well, fine. But I have to think now, don't I?"

Violet sighed. "Yes, being you, I guess so."

"Thanks," Andi said wryly.

"Oh, honey, I love you, but you really do think too much. Couldn't you just relax and enjoy it for a while?"

"No, because he doesn't want what I want."

"Not yet, anyway."

"Not ever, Vi." Andi had to remember that. No point in setting herself up for more crushing blows. She had to take what was left of their two weeks together and then turn her back on the past and force herself to find a future. A future that wouldn't include Mac. Damn it.

"What he wants," she said, "is to get me back into his bed and back to my job. I'm not even sure if that's the order he'd prefer it in."

"He just doesn't know what he really wants." Vi reached across the table and took Andi's hand. "It was the same with Rafe, I swear. Men can be completely clueless about this stuff. It's as if they can't admit to feeling more for a woman because it tears little chunks of their manhood off or something. But *love*, to most men, is a terrifying word. The big dummies."

"I don't know that Mac is scared of love, Vi," she said

after a moment's pause. "I just know that he doesn't feel it for me. He talked about being a great team. About how when I go back to the office, we can each have our own places and meet up for sex and nobody has to know."

"Oh, God." Vi's chin dropped to her chest. "I'm related to an idiot. It's mortifying."

Andi had to chuckle and it felt good, letting go a little of the misery crouched in the corner of her heart. Knowing Vi was on her side helped a lot. It just didn't change anything.

"I can't go back to work for him. And I've agreed to keep spending time with him until the two weeks are up, but how am I going to be able to stand it? It's not as if I can sleep with him again."

"Why the hell not?"

Andi laughed. "That's exactly what he said."

"For once, my brother was right. So why not?"

Andi took a drink of her tea to ease a suddenly desert-dry throat. "Because it'll only make it harder on me when it ends if I keep getting drawn into a fantasy that will never come true."

"You could make it true." Vi took another bite of her scone and moaned softly in appreciation.

"Fantasies, by their very definition, are just that."

"Doesn't mean you can't do something about them."

"Really?" Intrigued, Andi watched her friend's sly smile and felt only a small niggle of worry in reaction. "How?"

"Easy." Vi shrugged. "You have to dump him."

Andi blew out a pent-up breath. "Dump him? We're not together—how can I dump him?"

"You said it yourself. You spend time with him, but

you don't let him close. Do exactly what you were going to do. Don't sleep with him again. It'll drive him crazy."

Andi would like to think so, but Mac had an amazing ability to rebound from women. Why should she be any different from the legions he'd moved on from in the past?

"Think about it," Vi said. "What did Mac do when you quit your job?"

"Argued with me."

"Well, sure, but then?" She picked up her scone and gestured with it. "Mac went after you. Went to your house. Talked you into this two-week thing."

"True."

"Dump him and he'll come after you again," Violet pronounced. "I know my brother. And he won't be able to stand you walking away from him."

That did sound like Mac, Andi admitted. But coming after her because he didn't like to lose didn't mean anything, did it? That would just be him responding to a direct challenge. It wouldn't mean he cared. Briefly, she remembered how it had been between the two of them the night before and she felt a flush sweep over her in response. But letting herself be drawn into a wave of hope only to be crushed didn't sound appealing.

"I don't know," she said, shaking her head and breaking off another piece of her scone. "I'd be tricking him."

Violet gave a long, dramatic sigh. "And your point is?"

Andi laughed.

"All's fair in love and war, right?"

"He doesn't love me," Andi said.

"I wouldn't be so sure," Vi replied thoughtfully.

* * *

The Royal Diner was bustling with the usual lunch crowd, plus a handful of tourists thrown into the mix. Conversations flowed fast and furious, orders were called into the kitchen and the cook stacked finished meals on the counter, waiting for them to be picked up.

The place smelled like hamburgers and good, rich coffee and felt as comfortable as Mac's own living room. Which was why he didn't mind getting there early enough to snag a booth and people-watch until Rafe arrived.

Mac knew mostly everyone in town, really. It was nice to see Nolan and his wife, Raina, laughing together in a booth on the far side of the room. Then there were Joe Bennet and his foreman talking business over apple pie and coffee. And Sheriff Nathan Battle getting a kiss from his wife, Amanda, before taking his to-go lunch out the door with him.

Rafe came in as Nathan left, and Mac waved a hand in the air to get his friend's attention.

Sliding onto the bench seat opposite him, Rafe leaned back and said, "Thank you for the lunch invitation. I've been working since five this morning and really needed to take a break."

"Five?"

"Calls to London, Shanghai. You know how it is, dealing with international businesses."

"I do, but you know what? I've discovered something recently that you should try. Relaxing."

The other man laughed, set his phone on the table in front of him and signaled Amanda for a cup of coffee. "You are going to teach me how to relax? This is a joke, right?"

"No joke. Ironic, maybe. But not a joke." Mac glanced at his friend's phone. "You don't see me checking my phone, do you?"

Rafe frowned. "No, I do not. Where is it?"

"In the truck." Mac shrugged it off. "I'm learning to put the damn thing down. You should, too."

"Here you go, Rafe," Amanda said as she set the coffee in front of him. "What can I get you two?"

They ordered and when she moved off into the crowd again Rafe asked, "Just who is teaching you how to relax? Would it be Andrea?"

Mac nodded. "It would. Funny, but in the last few days, she's taught me a lot." Especially last night, he thought but didn't say. There were some things a man didn't talk about, even with his friends. What had happened between Andi and him was private and would remain that way.

"So Violet tells me. You're painting now? Repairing sinks and tile floors? Have you decided to go into the home construction business as a sideline?"

"Not exactly." Mac smiled when Amanda set his turkey sandwich in front of him and grabbed a french fry. Shaking it at Rafe, he said, "I'm helping her get her house into shape." *And stealing time with her.* "But being there with her, working alongside her, she's got me thinking."

"Please. Don't keep me waiting." Rafe took a bite of his fish sandwich and kept quiet.

"Okay. The way I see it, Andi and I are good together." He took a bite of his own sandwich, then added, "We've always worked well together and it turns out we're a great team...outside of the office, too."

Rafe lifted a dark eyebrow. "Go on."

"I want her." Three simple words that seemed to suddenly be filled with a lot more meaning than he'd expected. Yes, he wanted her back at the office, he wanted her back in his bed, but the bottom line was, he just *wanted* her. Period.

That thought was heavy enough to make him scowl down at his sandwich.

"You seem to have her," Rafe mused. "So what's the problem?"

"She's determined to back away, that's the damn problem." It irritated him to even say it. "I need to find a way to keep her."

"Do you love her?"

He jerked back. "No one said anything about love."

"Maybe you should."

Mac frowned at him. "You're feeling awful damn easy with that word. Not too long ago, it was different. You remember that?"

Rafe's eyes went dark. "Yes, all too well. I almost lost your sister to my own pride and stubborn refusal to see the truth of my own feelings. Will you let that happen to you as well, my friend? Or will you learn from my mistakes?"

"It's different," Mac insisted, grabbing a fry and popping it into his mouth. "You loved Violet."

"Well, if you do not love Andi, then let her go. Let her find a man who *will* love her as she deserves to be."

"What man?" Mac demanded, leaning over the table. "Is there some guy in town with his eye on Andi?"

Rafe blew out a laugh. "Any number of them, I should imagine. She's a lovely woman."

Scowling now, Mac snapped, "You're married to my sister, so you shouldn't be noticing things like that."

"I'm married, not dead."

"That could be arranged," Mac muttered, but Rafe only laughed.

"It seems to me that for a man who claims to not be in love, you're very territorial."

"I don't share," Mac grumbled. "Doesn't mean anything more than that."

"And so she should make herself available to you as your assistant, your mistress, your companion?"

Mac scowled again and couldn't find the appetite for more of his damn lunch. "Aren't you supposed to be on my side?"

"I am," Rafe assured him.

"Doesn't look like it from this side of the fence."

"I'm only trying to make you see that Andi deserves more than being your convenience."

"Never said she was convenient. A more argumentative woman I've never known. Except for my sister," he amended.

"I will agree that my wife is very opinionated."

Mac snorted a laugh. For all the times Rafe had made him furious over the years, for all the trouble he'd tried to stir up when he first blew into Royal, he was surely paying for it with the woman he loved. Violet had never been an easy woman, so Mac knew that Rafe's life was colorful, to say the least.

But Violet and Rafe were a team.

As he and Andi were. Or could be. If she would only see that he was right about this.

"You're walking a fine line here, Mac," Rafe said, taking a sip of his coffee. "If you step wrong, you could lose everything. I know."

Worry flickered in the back of his mind, but Mac

quashed it fast. There wasn't a damn thing Mac McCallum couldn't get once he'd made up his mind.

And his sights were set on Andi.

"I'll watch my step," he said, and picked up his sandwich again. "I know what I'm doing."

"I hope so, my friend," Rafe said with a shake of his head. "I do hope so."

Nine

Andi had never really planned to stay for so long, working for Mac.

When she started, it had seemed like a good place for her. After growing up in Royal, she'd left town, gone to college and, with her business degree, she'd headed to California. Working in LA had been exciting; living there had been less so. The crowds, the noise, the inability to look up at the sky and see more than a small square of smog-tinted blue had eventually begun wearing on her. At her core, she was a small-town girl and when she accepted that truth and moved back to Royal, things had fallen into place for her. She'd reconnected with her sister, found a fast and true friend in Violet and fallen stupidly in love with her boss.

"Okay, so not everything worked out," she muttered, setting some of her books onto the built-in shelves along one wall of her tiny living room. The house was coming together, the two weeks with Mac would soon be over and she had to do some thinking about her life.

The job with McCallum Enterprises had been good for her, though. She'd loved the energy, the rush of helping to run an international company with a great reputation. But it wasn't *hers*. Just like Mac, that company would never belong to her, and Andi wanted something of her own. To build a life and find what she was missing. To build a business from the ground up and watch it grow. She just didn't know what.

"Thank God you had tea made," Jolene said as she came into the living room carrying two tall ice-filled glasses with a small plate of cookies balanced on top of one of them. "I swear, summer's coming along too early for me."

"It's not that hot." Andi reached up to take the cookies and her glass of tea.

"Not in here, bless the air conditioning gods." Jolene eased down to the floor, maneuvering her belly as if it were a separate entity. "Oh, I should have gone shopping with you and Vi. It would have been much more relaxing, not to mention cooler. That baseball field will kill you. Blazing sun, the shouting, the crying—and that's just the parents…"

Andi laughed.

"Good," Jolene said with a brisk nod. "You can still do that."

"Of course I can. It's just, there's not a lot to laugh about right now."

"I could get Tom to go over and kick Mac's butt for you."

"No, but thanks for the thought."

Jolene shrugged. "Just as well. Tom really likes Mac."

"So do I." Andi grumbled as she bit into a cookie. "That's the problem."

"Damn it, I was so sure that once you'd had sex with the man it would either shatter your illusions or make him realize just how great you are. Numskull man."

"It's not his fault, Jolene," Andi said, taking a cookie she didn't really want and biting in, anyway. "I'm the one who fell in love."

"That's not a crime."

"No, but stupid should be."

"Honey, there aren't nearly enough jails if stupid turns out to be a crime."

"True." Taking a sip of her tea, Andi looked at her sister. "How did I live without you when I was in LA?"

"Beats hell out of me."

Andi grinned. "I was just sitting here thinking how glad I was that I moved back home. I've got you and Tom and your kids and I'll be here for the new baby's birth..."

"You bet you will. What if Tom gets called out to a fire? You're my backup."

Smiling still, Andi finished, "California just wasn't for me."

"No, but you figured that out, came home and found a job you loved. You'll do it again. As soon as you're ready."

"I think I am. Ready, I mean," Andi said as her idea solidified in her mind and settled in to stay. "But I've been doing a lot of thinking about this and I don't want a job, Jolene. I want my own business."

"Really? Great! What're you planning?"

"I'm going to be a professional organizer." It had been bumping along in her brain for a few months now and she'd toyed with it, even while she worked for Mac. She supposed that a part of her had realized that she couldn't stay at McCallum Enterprises forever, and her subconscious had been busily at work plotting her next move. She was going to organize people's homes, their businesses, heck, *garages*. She was great at finding order in chaos, so why shouldn't she make a living doing what she was so good at?

"That is the most brilliant idea you've had in years." Jolene had a wide smile on her face as she lifted her tea glass in a toast. "Honestly, I'll be your first customer. I'll expect the pregnant sister discount, of course, but you could come through and get my kids' bedrooms straightened out. Do you know I found an overlooked Easter egg in Jacob's room last week? I probably would have found it sooner, but I thought the smell coming from there was just from his discarded socks. Like usual."

Andi laughed. "Jacob's room may defeat me, but I'm willing to try."

"Then there's my kitchen and, God help you, Tom's workshop." Jolene reached out, took her sister's hand and squeezed. "It's a great idea and you'll be a huge success at it. Guaranteed."

"Thanks, I think I will, too. And God knows I've got the time to pour into it."

"But not like a workaholic again, right?" Concern shadowed Jolene's eyes briefly. "You're not going to turn into a stranger again while you bury yourself in work, right?"

"Absolutely. I want my own business," Andi said firmly, "but I want a *life*, too. And I'm going to find one, Jolene."

While her sister talked about the possibilities, Andi

thought about the night before, being in Mac's arms, the magic of the moment. A whisper of regret echoed in her heart, for all the hopes and dreams that would never be realized. Then she deliberately erased those images from her mind because it was time she started training herself to have that life she craved so much.

Without Mac.

The following day, Mac took her horseback riding.

She tried to regret agreeing to finish out the two weeks they'd originally decided on, but it wasn't easy. Because their remaining time together was really a gift to herself. When this time was up, Andi would have to walk away for her own sake, no matter what it might cost her. And in spite of what his sister might think or hope, Mac wouldn't follow her again. He didn't like losing.

These two weeks were his attempt to win her back. When that failed, Mac would move on—as he had so many times before.

Dumping him as Vi had suggested wouldn't work. And even if it would, Andi wasn't going to play games. If she had to trick Mac or trap him, he wouldn't be worth catching, would he? The heck of it was, Andi knew that if she told him the truth, admitted to loving him, it would throw him so hard, he'd walk away long before the two weeks were up. He wasn't interested in love.

But even knowing that she would be free of him if she just confessed, Andi couldn't do it. She still had her pride and damned if her last memory would be of Mac looking at her with pity shining in his eyes just before he turned away from her.

Those worries were for later. Today, they were here together, riding across open ranch land as if they were the only two people in the world. The Double M was a huge ranch, stretching out for miles. A stand of wild oaks straggled along the river and Mac led her in that direction. The sun was heating up and in another month, this ride would be downright miserable. But today was clear and just warm enough to remind you that summer was coming.

"You're thinking again," Mac said from beside her. "I can hear you from here."

"You've something against thinking?" She pulled the brim of her borrowed hat down lower over her eyes to cut the glare from the sun.

"On a day like today, while it's just us and the horses? Yeah, I do." He gave her a brief smile and nudged his horse closer to hers. "You know I didn't bring my phone with me?"

She laughed, delighted. So this time with her had changed him—if only a little. "I'm so proud."

"You should be," he said. "Without you, I'd be hunkered over in the saddle, checking stock reports, catching up with Tim and making sure Laura sent out the contracts due to be mailed today. Instead, thanks to you, I'm spending time on my ranch alongside a beautiful woman. And at the moment, I don't give two damns what's happening back at the office."

She smiled; how could she help it? The man was charming and darn near irresistible. Sadly, he knew it.

"So, are you going to show me where they set up the last water tank?"

"Interested in ranch life, are you?" The twinkle in his eye sparkled in the sunlight.

"Interested in seeing the tank I had to get road clearance approval on to bring in," she countered.

Ranchers kept huge water tanks stationed around their property to be filled by rainwater or, in times of serious drought, by water trucks brought in for that purpose. There were stock ponds, of course, natural watering holes for the animals, but they could go dry in a blistering hot Texas summer and you had to be able to refill them when necessary. The tanks were one sure way of accomplishing that. But several of them had come down during the big storm, and Mac had had to replace them. Now they were in place, only waiting to be filled before the start of summer.

Thankfully, they'd already had a good-sized storm at the beginning of the month and more were being predicted. In fact, she thought as she peered up at the sky to see gray-and-black clouds huddling together as if forming an attack strategy, it looked like another storm was headed this way so fast, Andi and Mac might get wet themselves before this ride was over.

"It's this way." He tugged on the reins and his horse moved in that direction. Nudging Apollo into a trot, Mac looked back to make sure Andi was following him. She was, and waved to him in reassurance. The gelding she rode was in no particular hurry, which was just as well. It had been a couple of years since she had been riding and she knew her muscles would be screaming by tomorrow.

Despite the heat of the sun, a brisk breeze blew, bringing the scent of the storm with it. Andi pulled her hat down hard so it wouldn't blow away and followed after Mac, determined to keep up. It was another twenty minutes to the stock pond and the water tank that stood alongside it.

"The pond looks good." She dismounted with a quiet sigh of relief.

"It's early yet," Mac said, squinting into the sun, watching a few lazy cattle meander down to the water's edge for a drink. "But yeah. Last year, the water level was only half as much at this point in the season. A couple more good storms," he said, checking out the sky, "and we'll be set. Tanks and ponds."

"It's a lot, Mac," she said softly, letting her gaze sweep across miles of grazing land. Cattle dotted the countryside, and here and there a few horses were sprinkled in as added interest. "Running your business, and the ranch, it's a lot. Do you ever want to hand the reins over to someone else? Step back from it?"

For a second, it looked as though he might give her a wink and a grin and the kind of quick, smooth answer he was best known for. But then his features evened out and he took another long look around him before turning back to her. "No. I don't. Though I'll say, if I ever had to make a choice—either the business or the ranch—the ranch would win hands down." He bent over, scooped up a handful of dirt and grass and then turned his hand over, letting it all drift to earth again. "I love this place. Every blade of grass and clod of dirt. Every stupid steer, every irritation. The worry about not enough water, too much water, calves being born, losing some to coyotes…" He stood up again and shook his head. "It's McCallum land and I guess it's in me."

She heard it in his voice, saw it in his eyes. The business he'd taken over when his parents died was something he'd built, defined, expanded because he'd needed to prove something. To his father. Himself. Maybe even the world. But this ranch was the soul of him. What kept him going, what drove him. His love for the land and the continuity of caring for it.

Her heart turned over in her chest as he looked at her, and Andi wondered how much more she could possibly love him. How could the feeling inside her keep growing, filling her up until she thought she must be glowing with it?

He tipped his head to one side, stared at her. "What is it? You've got this weird expression your face."

She smiled and walked toward him. Just when she thought she had come to grips with everything, he threw her for a loop again. Seeing him like this, standing tall and arrogant and proud on land his family had owned for generations, made her want to tell him everything. Confess her love, let him know what she thought and felt. She couldn't, though, any more than she could turn from him now and pretend she'd heard and felt nothing.

"You just…surprise me sometimes, that's all," she said, walking close enough that she could reach up and cup his cheek in her palm. Heat flowed from his body to hers and back again. "You're kind of wonderful."

Pleasure shone in his eyes. He covered her hand with his and, as their gazes locked, she felt a shift in the emotions charging around them. Passion burned just beneath the surface, a reminder that what was between them was powerful, difficult to ignore or deny.

"If I'd known it would have this effect on you," he whispered, "I'd have brought you out to the water tank before."

She laughed and shook her head. "You're also impossible."

"So it's been said." He pulled her in close until she had to tip her head back to look up at him.

"What am I doing here?" she murmured, more to herself than to him.

He took her hat off, smoothed her hair back from her face, dipped his head and whispered, "Driving me crazy."

Lightning flashed in the distance and thunder rolled toward them like an approaching army. Then he kissed her and the storm erupted around them, pelting them with rain they didn't even notice.

When the storm rushed in and lightning began to slash at the ground much closer to them, they broke apart and climbed onto the horses.

Drenched and laughing like loons, they outpaced the storm, rode up to the ranch house and turned the horses over to the stable hands. Then racing for the house, Mac and Andi ran into the kitchen and gratefully took the towels Teresa offered them.

"Couple of crazy people is what you are," she muttered, with a half smile tugging at her lips. Her short, gray-streaked brown hair hugged her head like a cap. Her lipstick was bright red and her nails were painted to match. She wore jeans, boots and a long-sleeved blue-and-white-checked shirt. "Could have been struck by lightning out in this storm. You're lucky you're just half-drowned instead."

"Thank you, Teresa," Andi said, running the towel over her hair and toeing her boots off one at a time. "We're messing up your floor. I'm so sorry."

Mac glanced behind them and saw the muddy footprints and small river of water that had followed them in. He cringed a little and added his own apology. He might own the house, but Teresa ruled it, and everyone on the ranch knew it. "We gave you more work to do, didn't we?"

Impatiently, Teresa waved that away. "Don't have

nearly enough to do around here to keep me busy, so don't worry about that. You two go on up now and get out of those wet clothes. I'll throw everything in the dryer as soon as you do."

"I'll bring our clothes down in a couple minutes." Barefoot now, Mac took Andi's hand and pulled her along with him, though she came reluctantly. He had to assume it was because she was embarrassed that Teresa knew the two of them would soon be naked together. But she'd just have to get over that or risk pneumonia. Already, she was shivering from the effects of being soaking wet and the air conditioning blowing through the house. So reluctant or not, she followed after him, down the hall, up the stairs and to his bedroom.

"Come on, get out of those wet clothes," he urged as he stripped himself.

"You're just trying to get me out of my panties again." Her voice trembled with cold.

"You caught on to my nefarious scheme. Make a woman so damn cold she turns blue, then have my way with her."

She laughed shortly. Her hands shook as she undid buttons and then pulled off her shirt, jeans and underwear. He tried not to look because the point here was getting her warm again, not jumping her the minute she was vulnerable. Once they were both finished, he tossed her his robe, then pulled on a pair of dry jeans without bothering with boxers beneath them.

Bundling up the sodden mess of clothes, he opened the bedroom door. "I'll just take these to Teresa and be right back."

"Take your time. This is so humiliating," she murmured, sitting on the edge of his bed, shaking her head.

"Yeah, getting caught in a storm is a real embarrassment." He grinned at her then bolted back down the stairs. He knew she wasn't going anywhere, but he wanted to get back to her quickly.

Teresa was waiting for him. "I'll get those dry. You take up that tray I fixed for the two of you. Get some of that hot coffee into Andi before she turns into an icicle."

"I will." Mac spotted the tray on the kitchen table and couldn't stop the smile of appreciation. There was leftover fried chicken, potato salad, a half-dozen cookies, two mugs and a small carafe of coffee.

Impulsively, he kissed her cheek and was shocked to see her blush. "You are a wonder," he said softly. "And I don't think I tell you that often enough. Thanks, Teresa. I appreciate it."

"Well, now, you two need some warming up—and food and coffee are just one of the ways to get that done." She slid him a sly smile. "I imagine you can think of another way."

He winked at her. "Oh, one or two come to mind."

Back upstairs, he found Andi just where he'd left her. Her hair was dark and wet and she was looking a little less sure of herself, which was, he told himself, a good thing. He wanted her as off balance as he'd been lately. Damn it, all he could think about was her. From the first day of their two-week agreement, she'd been front and center in his mind. And if anything, it had only gotten worse the more time they spent together. Her laugh haunted him, her eyes filled his dreams and the scent of her seemed to always be in the air. Andi had somehow become a part of him and he wasn't quite sure what to do about that.

Oh, he'd once thought about a future wife and children

in a vague, maybe-one-day kind of way. But that was a long time ago. Before he'd had responsibility thrust on him by his parents' deaths.

Then it had been not only the family ranch—that had been in McCallum hands for generations—and the business his father had been building, but there had also been Violet, his teenage sister he had to protect and look after. He and Vi had butted heads time and again, which was to be expected, but being brother *and* father to her had made keeping their relationship tight that much harder.

So he'd buried himself in work because at least there, he was sure of his footing. Slowly, over time, he'd lost all sense of a future because his present was packed with far too much already.

Mac's parents had been happy. He and Vi had been raised by people who loved each other and them. But when they died, it was as if Mac had shut down that loving side of himself. The part that remembered family and laughter and the ease of just being happy. He hadn't had time for happiness back then. It had all been about saving his father's company. Keeping the ranch together. Diversifying. Building on a fortune to make sure that Violet would never have to worry. He'd expanded the ranch beyond his father's dreams and he'd built a company that was larger and more successful than anyone could have imagined. And somewhere along the line, he realized, he'd lost himself.

In the past ten days or so, he'd begun to find the man he used to be. He'd laughed more, talked more and done less work than he had in ten years. But who he was now was ingrained in his soul. Wasn't it too late to go backward? To try to reclaim permanently the younger version of himself? The one that had plans beyond running a successful company? If he tried, didn't he run the risk of losing everything he'd built?

"Mac?" Andi's voice cut into his thoughts and brought him back from the meandering road his mind had taken. "You okay?"

"Yeah," he said, focusing on her and letting the rest go. For now, anyway. "Fine. Look. I bring supplies."

She smiled. "I can't imagine what Teresa's thinking right now."

"I can." He grinned and carried the tray to the table set between the two cozy chairs in front of the hearth. "She's thinking, *Look at all that mud and water. He's a lucky man to have a girl like Andrea Beaumont give him a second glance when he drags her through a thunderstorm on horseback.*"

Andi laughed as he'd meant her to.

"Come over here," he urged. "I'm gonna start a fire, get us both warmed up while we eat."

She stood up and he saw she was dwarfed by his dark red robe. The hem of it hung to well below her knees and her hands had disappeared into the sleeves. But she didn't look as pale and cold as she had before. While she took a seat, picked up one of the coffee mugs and took a sip, Mac built a fire in the hearth.

He supposed it really wasn't cold enough to warrant it. And it was completely illogical to have a fire going while the air conditioner was running. But the flames already licking at the kindling and snapping up along the stacked logs were comforting. Romantic. With a naked Andi within arm's reach, romantic was a very good thing.

"I love a fireplace," she said softly, staring at the blaze as the flickering light washed over her features. "I wish my house had one."

He took the chair beside hers, relishing the feel of the heat rushing toward him from the hearth. "Feel free to come and use mine any time you want."

"Thanks." She tipped her head to one side and smiled at him. "Maybe I will."

They ate cold chicken and talked about the town, their families, their friends, studiously avoiding all mention of what was between them. Tension coiled in the air and snapped as hungrily as the flames on wood.

By unspoken agreement, they hadn't had sex since that first time, but whenever he tried to sleep, Mac relived that night over and over again. The taste of her. The feel of her beneath his hands. The hot damp core of her that took him in and held him. Before Andi, after he'd had a woman, she retreated from his mind, as if with the need satisfied, he was content to move on to whatever—or whoever—came next.

With Andi, though, it was just the opposite. He wanted his hands on her again. Wanted to lay claim to all that she was. Wanted to hear her sighs and watch those storm-gray eyes of hers glaze over with passion then flash with completion when he took her.

Hell. He just *wanted* her. All the damn time. More than his next breath. More than anything.

"Um," she said, as if reading his mind and the quick, hungry thoughts racing through it, "we should see if our clothes are dry. Or maybe I could borrow something of yours just to get home in and—"

She was backing away. Sitting right there beside him and pulling back from him and he wasn't going to let her. Need drove him out of his chair. Want had him kneeling on the floor in front of her, staring up into gray eyes that would, he was sure, continue to haunt him for years to come.

"Or," Mac said, as he came up on his knees, "there are other options."

She took a deep breath and shook her head, making her still-damp hair swing about her face. "Mac, we shouldn't—"

"Miss a golden opportunity," he finished for her. Reaching out, he untied the robe belt at her waist, then spread the fabric apart. She shivered and her eyes went glassy as his hands skimmed over her body with sure, long strokes.

"Oh, Mac…"

She sighed and he knew he had her. Knew she wouldn't say no, wouldn't turn away from what they could find together. Running his hands up her body, he cupped her breasts and pulled gently at her rigid nipples. He loved watching that dazed expression come into her eyes. Loved the sound of her breath hitching in her lungs. Loved…

He parted her thighs, spreading her legs wide, then leaned in, covered her with his mouth and devoured her. Her quick gasp of surprise, then desperation, filled his head. Her sighs, her whimpers, her jerky movements as he pleasured her body, fed him, pushed him on. He licked, nibbled, suckled at her until she lifted her hips off the chair and threaded her fingers through his hair, holding his head to her as her cries became pleas.

She was frantic now for what he could give her and her need fueled his own. She cried out his name and the sound became a choked-off scream of release as the first explosions rocketed through her.

He continued to push, to torment her even as her body

splintered in his grasp. And before the last of the tremors shook her, he pulled her from the chair, laid her out on the rug in front of the fire and buried himself deep inside her.

The tight, damp heat of her surrounded him, and Mac paused long enough to savor the sensation of being close enough to become a part of her. He threw his head back and practically roared his satisfaction. Then she moved, arching into him, rocking her hips, urging him on.

"More, Mac," she whispered harshly. "Give me more. *Take* more of me." Her head tipped back, exposing the line of her throat, and he tucked his face into that curve, kissing her, feeling the beat of her heart in the pulse that pounded against his mouth.

His mind fogged, his heart raced. Together they rushed to completion, bodies joined in an ancient dance that felt new and wondrous. All other thoughts fled, dissolving in the wide, deep ocean of sensation they were sinking into. He felt her body tighten around his, her legs lock around his middle and even as she called his name brokenly, he joined her in the fall, giving her everything he was.

Ten

It wasn't until later, as they lay wrapped together in a blissful haze, that Mac suddenly snapped back to reality. When he realized what had just happened, he groaned, closed his eyes and muttered, "Damn it."

"What?" It came on a sigh, as if she really couldn't bring herself to care what was wrong. She slid one hand down his back and her touch felt like fire-wrapped velvet.

No way to do this an easy way. Just say it. Lifting his head, he stared down into her eyes and said, "I didn't use protection."

Well, he thought, watching her eyes flash wide with apprehension, that was dropping a lead balloon on the festivities.

"Oh, God." She covered her eyes with one hand.

He pulled away from her but didn't move far. Her skin

gleamed like fine porcelain in the firelight. Her eyes flashed and changed as emotions, like the firelit shadows, danced in them. "My fault," he said tightly. "Can't believe I did that. It's never happened before. Swear to God, you are the only woman I've ever met who could shut down my brain so completely."

She worked up a pitiful smile at that halfhearted compliment. She sat up, grabbed her blanket and drew it around her shoulders before huddling deeply into it.

"It's okay," she said firmly, as if trying to convince herself as well as him. "It was just the once. I'm sure it's fine."

Mac snorted, disgusted with himself for losing control and amused at her attempt at a positive attitude. "Yeah, I'm guessing couples have been telling each other that for centuries."

"Couples?" she repeated softly, then shook her head. "Doesn't matter. It's fine, I'm sure."

Couples. Was that what they were? For so long, they'd been colleagues. Boss and assistant. Friends. Had they worked around to where they were a couple now? When did that happen? What the hell should he do about it?

Too many things to think about when most of his blood supply was situated well below his brain. "We'll find out soon enough, won't we?" He propped his back against the closest chair, then dragged her up next to him despite her attempt to squirm away. She was stiff with tension, and he knew her mind had to be racing through every imaginable scenario and there was nothing he could do to make it easier.

He stared into the fire and tried to do some thinking of his own. The first rush of panic and self-directed fury was easing now, and Mac indulged himself in exploring a few of those future possibilities. If Andi wasn't pregnant, they could go on as they always had. Surprisingly enough, that notion wasn't as appealing as it had been even two short weeks ago.

If there was no baby and she still wanted to quit her job, he'd have to find a way to deal with that. He couldn't force her to stay if she was determined to leave. Mac frowned at the fire as Andi shifted in his grasp, probably uneasy with her thoughts. And he really couldn't blame her.

If she was pregnant, well, that opened up a whole new road. She would be carrying *his* child, so she wouldn't be walking away from him no matter what she wanted to believe.

A baby. He rubbed one hand across his face, took a deep breath and released it slowly, waiting for another wave of panic.

It didn't come.

Hell, he thought, if Andi was pregnant, she'd marry him, live here at the ranch. They'd work together, raise their kid and have great sex. The two of them would have the best of all possible worlds. That sounded pretty good to him.

The hard part would be hog-tying her until she agreed with him.

"Mac?"

"Yeah?" He tightened his hold on her in case she tried to bolt.

But she only turned her face up to his, her gray eyes stormy. "This doesn't change anything between us. It can't."

He tucked her head onto his shoulder, rested his chin on top of her head and stared into the fire blazing in the river-stone hearth. "Guess we're gonna find out about that, aren't we?"

A few days later, they still hadn't really talked about what had happened and the possible repercussions. Andi simply refused to think about it because she knew that if a part of her would really love to be pregnant with Mac's baby—it would never happen. If she were terrified at the possibility, it was almost guaranteed she'd be pregnant.

That's just the way life worked and she accepted it.

Mac, though, had been acting differently for days. She couldn't really identify what he was thinking, but she knew there was a change in him. Was it panic at the thought of perhaps being a father? Or was it something…else?

A flutter of hope tangled with anticipation in the pit of her stomach. Maybe he had come to care for her. Maybe he was looking at what the two of them had and seeing it for what it could be. Maybe.

"I bring pizza," he announced as he came in from her kitchen. He was balancing a large butcher-block cutting board that held a steaming sausage-and-mushroom pie.

All day, they'd worked on the pink room, with Mac helping the appliance delivery guy install her new black-and-chrome range. They'd tried out her new oven with a bake-it-yourself pizza she'd picked up at the market, and judging by the delicious scents wafting to her, it had worked great.

Smiling in spite of the turmoil bubbling inside her, Andi held up two glasses of dark red wine. "And I've already poured, so that's great timing."

He frowned a little as he set the pizza down on her tiny coffee table. "Maybe you shouldn't be drinking wine."

Andi sighed. "I'm not pregnant, Mac."

"We don't know that."

"Well, until we do, cheers." One glass wasn't going to hurt her or the baby if there was one. And being here with Mac, in the twilight of an early summer evening, she needed the wine.

He shrugged, served them each a slice and handed her a plate as he took a seat beside her on the floor. Andi took a bite, then waved a hand at her mouth in an attempt to cool it off.

"Yep," he said, "new oven works great. What's convection?"

"I should know that," she admitted as she huffed out a breath trying to cool the molten cheese currently burning the roof of her mouth. "But I don't."

"That makes me feel better," he admitted with a grin. Taking a sip of his wine, he looked around the living room. "We did a really good job in here, didn't we?"

"We did."

"Great team."

"Don't start."

"I'm not starting," he told her with a wink, "I'm continuing. There's a difference."

Mac being charming was hard to resist, and still, she had to. She picked up her wine for a sip.

"Andi, we've got something great." His gaze locked on to hers. "Don't walk away from it."

Sighing a little, she shook her head. "I told you, Mac, I can't keep working for you. I want a life."

"Well, so do I now." He set his glass down, then

plucked hers from her hand and set it aside, too. Taking her hands in his, he rubbed his thumbs across her knuckles while he looked deeply into her eyes. "Over the last couple of weeks, I've discovered a few things."

That flutter of hope beat a little faster in her stomach. "Such as?"

Nodding, he said, "Such as, I forgot just how good it felt to take my horse out and ride the ranch myself instead of just relying on reports from my foreman."

"I'm glad." Remembering the look on his face when he told her about what the ranch meant to him, she smiled. Maybe she had gotten through to him. At least a little.

"And," he added with a quick grin, "I learned that not answering my phone doesn't mean instant death."

Laughing, she said, "Also good."

"Mostly, though," he said, and his voice dropped to a low, throaty hush that seemed to ripple along her nerve endings, "I learned what we have."

"Mac—"

"Just wait," he said and held on to her hands when she tried to tug free. "Look, I admit, I was doing all of this to get you to come back to the office. Couldn't see how I'd run the place without you. But it's more now."

There went that flutter of hope again. "More?" She held her breath, watched his eyes.

"We're great together." He said it flatly, brooking no argument even if she'd been inclined to try. "Hell, we have *fun* together. The sex is incredible and damn it, Andi, if we can have it all, why shouldn't we?"

And the hope died.

This was only what he'd said before. Teamwork. Come

back to the office. Be his trusty sidekick. Keep separate homes. Have sex with him. Don't let anyone know.

"If it turns out you are pregnant," he was saying, and Andi warned herself to pay attention, no matter what pain it cost, "we can get married and live out at the ranch." He gave her that smile filled with charm as if that would be enough to smooth over the jagged edges of her heart. "Closer commute for both of us. And Teresa's there to take care of the baby while we're at work."

The last remaining remnants of that hope burned to a cinder and the ashes blew away.

God, she was an idiot.

Before she could tell him to leave, his phone rang. "You mind?" he asked after glancing at the readout.

"No, go ahead." It would give her another moment or two to find the right words to end this. God. How could she be so cold?

"Right… Okay, Tim… Yeah, I know you could. But I'll feel better if I meet you. Twenty minutes?" He hung up, slid the phone into his pocket and looked at Andi. "We've got to finish this later. I have to get to the office. The Brinkman deal is faltering."

Brinkman. She flipped through her mental files. "Oh. Brinkman Auto Industries."

"Right." He stood up, then leaned over and took a last bite of his now cool pizza. Still chewing, he told her, "There are a few things to be done before Hal Brinkman panics and backs out entirely."

"Why are you going in?" Sitting on the floor, she stared up at him and said, "Tim was point person on that deal. No one knows Brinkman better than he does."

"Yeah, but it's my company. Buck stops with me." He narrowed his eyes on her. "And you. Come to the office with me, Andi. You did all the prelim work on those contracts. With your mind, you remember every single detail."

Her heart actually *hurt*. "No, Mac."

Frowning, he stared at her. "What do you mean, 'no'?"

"I mean, I quit, Mac. Two weeks ago. And if that doesn't help, I quit again. This time, it's final." Mac was ready to race out the door even though this wasn't an emergency. Andi had to recognize that she simply wasn't a priority to him. Never would be.

How could he not see it? Despite everything they'd shared the past two weeks, nothing had changed. He wanted her. Back in the office. Back in his bed. And for nothing else. It hurt to accept. To realize that Mac hadn't changed. Not really. His company was still the most important thing to him.

Even now, when he was trying to finagle her back into his life, he was willing to put that conversation on hold so he could race to the office to deal with something his vice president was completely capable of handling.

"I'm done, Mac." Slowly, Andi stood up, because if she was going to stand her ground metaphorically, then she'd do it literally, too. "You're running back to the office when they don't even need you to."

"It's business," he said as if that explained everything.

"And Tim can handle it, but you won't let him. You have to be there." She shook her head sadly and looked at him as if etching this memory into her mind forever. It would help, she told herself, while she worked to get over him. "I thought your heart was really in the ranch, but I was wrong. It's in that office. In the computers and the files and the phone calls and hustle of the day. But mine's not, Mac. It's not what I want."

"What the hell *do* you want, Andi?"

She laughed quietly, sadly. "I want Easter eggs that smell like little boys' sweaty socks. I want little girls who have tea parties with their hamsters. Little League games and cheerleading practice."

He looked so confused, it broke her heart. He'd never understand so she wouldn't bother trying to explain.

"Mostly, I want love, Mac. I want to be loved like I love you."

"You—" His head jerked back as if she'd slapped him.

"Yeah," she said softly, sadly, as hope dissolved into dead dreams and left her feeling hollowed out from the inside. She'd had to say it, if only once. She didn't want his pity, but damn it, she deserved the opportunity to tell the man she loved him, even if she shouldn't. "But don't hold it against me. I'll get over it eventually."

"What the hell am I supposed to do with that?"

"If you have to ask," she said, "then I can't explain it."

"Okay." He shook his head, hard. "Leaving that aside for a second, you've known me long enough that you should understand what that company means to me. Hell, it meant a lot to you, too, once."

It had. But those days were gone. "Not as much as having a life, Mac. That means more."

"So you can just walk away? From me? From what we've had for years? What we had the last two weeks?"

"I have to," she said simply.

"You love me so much you can't get away fast enough?" He laughed shortly and there was fury and pain shining in his eyes. "What the hell kind of love is that?"

She sighed and her heart broke a little more. "The kind I can recover from. I hope."

* * *

The next two weeks were a lot less interesting than the previous ones. Mac fell back on his default settings and buried himself in work. The office. The ranch. He kept himself so damn busy he didn't have time to sleep. Because he couldn't risk dreaming.

Tim was now generally stationed at the office and working with Laura to run down new leads on failing companies that might be suitable takeover material. The Brinkman contract problems had been solved readily enough and looking back Mac could see that Andi had been right. Tim could have handled it. But the point was, this was Mac's business and his responsibility. So of course he'd had to go in. Supervise. Give his opinion and monitor the situation until it was settled. There was zero reason for him to feel guilty about doing what he had to.

So why did he?

She loved him.

A cold, tight fist squeezed his heart. Why the hell would she tell him that and then toss him out of her damn house? That was love? He rubbed at the center of his chest as if he could ease the ache that had settled in there the night he'd last walked away from Andi's house.

She loved him.

Well, if she loved him, why wasn't she *there*? You can't say you love someone and then say, *But I don't like you doing this and this. You should do that instead.* What the hell kind of love was that?

He kept remembering Andi's face, the expression in her eyes. The…disappointment he'd read there. And he didn't like it. Didn't care to remember that she'd told him to leave. That he'd never change. Hell, he had changed.

He'd asked her to come back to work for him, hadn't he? He hadn't demanded it.

Pushing up out of his chair, Mac paced the confines of his office like a tiger looking for an escape route out of his cage. That thought brought him up short. Made him frown as he looked out the window to a wide sweep of McCallum land. The office wasn't a cage. It was… what? The heart of him, as Andi had said?

"No, damned if it is," he muttered. Stalking to the window, he slapped both hands on either side of the glass and leaned toward it.

Outside, the sun was heating up. July was just around the corner and summer was settling in to stay for a while. On the ranch, they'd be moving the herd to a new pasture. The sky looked brassy and there wasn't a cloud in sight. But he didn't really care what kind of view he was staring at. "Why the hell is she being so stubborn?"

He missed her, damn it. What did sweaty Easter eggs have to do with anything?

"That's it, you're gonna snap soon. Talking to yourself." He shoved away from the window and went back to pacing. "You start answering your own questions and you're done, son."

He kicked his desk and gritted his teeth against the pain. He didn't want to miss her, but he couldn't deny that without Andi in his life, it felt as though he was missing a limb.

He'd interviewed a half dozen people for the executive assistant job and not one of them had been able to read his mind the way Andi could. Being at the office wasn't enjoyable anymore. He didn't want to be here, but he couldn't find any damn peace at his own house, either.

Every time he walked in the door, Teresa gave him a cool, disapproving look. And when he tried to sleep in his own bed, visions of Andi rose up and kept sleep at bay while his body burned. He couldn't even look at the hearth in his room without remembering those moments in the firelight with Andi. She'd changed everything on him. And now it felt as if nothing fit quite right.

The buzzer on his desk phone sounded and he glared at it. No damn peace. Three long strides had him at his desk. He hit a button and snapped, "What is it?"

"Sorry, Mac," Laura said coolly and he winced in response. "Tim's on line one."

"Fine. Thanks." His vice president was in Northern California to foster a deal on a tech company. Mac picked up, turned to look out the window again and said, "Yeah, Tim. How's it going?"

"Not good." Tim sounded hesitant—the kind of tone people used when they were about to break bad news and really wished they didn't have to. "Jackson Tully made a deal with someone else last week. We lost out, Mac. Sorry, there was nothing I could do. Tully wanted his business to stay in California."

Mac heard but was barely listening. He realized that a couple of months ago, that news would have made him furious. They'd put in a lot of time, working up strategies for the Tully takeover. The tech company was on its last legs and Mac had figured to pick it up cheap, restructure, then sell it for a profit within eighteen months. Now that plan was shot.

And he didn't care. Scrubbing one hand across the back of his neck, he acknowledged that the blown deal didn't mean anything to him. Because Andi wasn't there. She was gone so nothing else mattered.

What the hell had she done to him?

He rubbed his eyes. "It's all right, Tim. Come on home. Time to move on to something else."

"If it's okay with you," he said, "I'll stay a couple more days. Have a lead on a sinking computer company. I figure it's worth a look."

"Sure. Keep me posted."

Mac hung up, thinking that a month ago, he'd have been all over that news, eager to carve another notch in McCallum Enterprises' belt.

But what the hell did success mean when you didn't have anyone to share it with? When you didn't have the *one* person who mattered. Always before, he and Andi had celebrated every deal together, congratulated each other on the maneuvering, the planning and the final win.

But she was gone and he'd just have to get the hell over it. He wasn't going to go after her again. A man had to hang on to some of his pride, didn't he?

"I didn't know I could be this bored." Andi slumped into one of her new kitchen chairs and propped both elbows on the table. Staring at Vi, she said, "The house is painted. The new furniture's here. There's nothing left for me to *do*."

"What about starting your business?" Vi asked, reaching for an Oreo. "Isn't that on the agenda?"

"It should be," Andi mused, turning her coffee cup around and around between her palms. "But there's no hurry and I'm just not feeling real motivated, you know?"

It had been three weeks since Mac walked out of her house for the last time. July had arrived and her sister was insisting she attend the Royal Fourth of July celebration. She couldn't have felt less like being around people who would expect her to smile and mean it.

Violet sighed, dunked her cookie in her coffee and said, "Mac is being stupid."

"He's being Mac."

"That's what I said." Vi bit her cookie and muffled a groan.

Andi laughed a little, but her heart wasn't in it. Those two weeks with Mac had gone too quickly. She'd thought she was building memories, but what she'd really constructed were personalized torture devices. Whenever she closed her eyes, he was there. How was she supposed to get over him, get past this feeling, when her own subconscious was working against her?

She had to find a way because Andi knew Mac wouldn't be coming back. She'd done the unthinkable and told him no. He'd let her go and called it a lesson learned, because his pride wouldn't allow him to come for her again.

"You know," Vi spoke up again. "Mac's just as miserable as you are."

"He is?" Ridiculous how that thought cheered her up. It seemed misery did love company after all.

"That's got to make you feel a little better."

"It does." Andi got up, went to her new French-door refrigerator and got more tea to refill their glasses. "But you know, rather than the two of us being sad and gloomy apart, I'd rather we were happy. Together." She poured the tea, offered her friend more Oreos, then said, "But it's over, Vi. I can't go back to the office. I love him, so working with him every day would be a nightmare. And I can't jump back into his bed—same reason. The problem is, I haven't figured out yet how I'm supposed to live without him."

"I don't think you're going to have to," Vi said quietly.

Andi looked at her. "Why?"

Smiling, Vi said, "If there's one thing I know, it's my brother. Mac loves you, sweetie. He just hasn't figured it out yet."

"I wish I could believe that." Andi shook her head, and lifted her chin. She had to protect herself. She couldn't keep building hopes on a shaky foundation and not expect them to crash down around her. So instead of giving in to the urge to pin her dreams on Vi's words, Andi said quietly, "I can't take the chance, Vi. I can't wait and hope and keep my fingers crossed. I love Mac, but I'm not going to put my life on hold just on the chance he might wake up and realize that he loves me."

"Oh, Andi…"

"No." Taking a deep breath, Andi said, "Living without him will be the hardest thing I've ever had to do. But I've got to find a way to do it."

Eleven

Mac was working a horse in the corral when his sister found him. He was in no mood for company. Hell, hadn't he bolted from the office because he wanted to be left alone? Feeling surly, he dismounted, tossed the reins to the nearest ranch hand and crossed the dirt enclosure to where his sister waited just outside the fence.

The heat was steaming, making him even more irritable, which he wouldn't have believed possible. Snatching his hat off, he raked his fingers through his hair, then slapped the brim of the hat against his jeans to get rid of at least some of the dirt he'd managed to collect. He opened the gate, stepped through and secured it again. Only then did Mac look at his sister.

"Violet, what are you doing here?"

"It's still my home as much as yours," she reminded him.

"Bet that's news to Rafe." He tugged his hat back on. "Go home, Violet."

"Not until we have a talk," she said.

"Not in the mood."

"Too bad."

"Not a good day for this, Violet." He turned and headed for the stable, but she was right behind him, though she had to hurry her steps just to keep up.

"Pregnant here, not as fast as I used to be," she called out, and that made him stop. He couldn't risk her falling and injuring herself or the baby.

He faced her, his arms crossed over his chest, feet planted wide apart. Squinting into the sun, he glared at her. "Fine. Talk."

"What is wrong with you?" she demanded.

He gritted his teeth and sucked air in through his nose. His temper was dangerously close to erupting so he made a deliberate attempt to hold it down. "Not a damn thing except for an interfering little sister."

Poking her index finger against his chest, she asked, "Don't you see that Andi is the best thing that ever happened to you?"

Of course he saw that. Was he blind? But Andi was the one who'd ended things. "If that's all you came to talk about, this meeting is over."

Damned if he'd stand here and be lectured to by his younger sister. He had stuff to do. And he figured if he kept himself busy enough, he wouldn't have the room or the time to think about Andi.

"You're an idiot."

Mac shook his head. He'd had about enough of women lately. "Great. Thanks for stopping by. Say hi to Rafe."

"I'm not done."

"Yeah," he nearly growled. "You're done. I don't want to share my feelings, Vi. I'm not looking for a soft shoulder or a stern talking-to. You can butt the hell out because this is none of your business, understand?"

"We're *family*, you knot-head," she snapped, and leading with her prodigious belly, encroached on his personal space. "If you think you can scare me off with that nasty streak of yours, you can forget it. I'm only here because I love you."

He had already been pushed way past the edge of his control. The woman he wanted insisted she loved him, but didn't want him. His company didn't interest him. He couldn't even work up any concentration for the horses he loved. The heat was boiling his brain and his little sister dropping in to insult him was just the icing on his damn cake.

Scrubbing his hand through his hair, he muttered darkly, "Suddenly I've got women who love me giving me nothing but grief."

"That's right. Andi *loves* you. What're you going to do about it?"

He frowned at her, eyes narrowing in suspicion. "Does Rafe know you have Oreo breath?"

Vi jerked back, looked embarrassed, then shook it off and argued, "This isn't about me."

One eyebrow lifted. "So my life is up for grabs, but yours is private?"

"Yes," Vi said, lifting her chin to glare at him. "Because I'm not currently being an idiot."

Mac scowled at her. "You're not exactly endearing yourself to me."

Sighing, Violet moved in closer, gave him a hard hug and whispered, "I love you, Mac. I want you happy. So I'm asking you to try some personal growth. Fast."

He hugged her back, then released her. "It's over, Vi. Let it go."

"She's pregnant," Violet blurted out.

"What?"

"Andi. She's pregnant."

Ears ringing, heart slamming in his chest, Mac was staggered. Pregnant? Why hadn't she told him? What the hell kind of love was it that made you leave *and* hide a child? Breath caught in his chest until it felt as if he might just explode. Instantly, images, thoughts, emotions chased each other through his mind. Panic was there, naturally, along with pride, excitement, anger and a sense of satisfaction. Pregnant. Andi was carrying his child. His baby.

Mac examined exactly what he was feeling and realized the one underlying emotion that was strongest was also the most unfamiliar. Happiness. Hell, it had been so long since he'd really been completely happy, no wonder he hardly recognized it.

"Mac? You okay?"

He came up out of his thoughts like a diver breaking the water's surface. "I'm better than okay."

Giving his sister a hard kiss, he grinned at her and said, "This may never be true again, so listen up. Thank you for interfering. For sticking your nose in. For loving me."

Violet smiled up at him. "It was my pleasure."

"I know it."

"So, since you're so grateful to me, we don't have to say anything to Rafe about the cookies, right?"

He only smiled. He loved her, but his little sister could just go home and worry that she'd be ratted out. It would do her good. Leaving her there by the corral, he headed

for the house. He had to change, get to town, then go see
the woman who was currently driving him nuts.

Andi couldn't take boredom for long. By the following day, she had been to the Royal nursery and come
home with a plan.

She had a half-dozen bags of red cedar mulch, flats
of petunias and gerbera daisies and a few bags of peat
moss. She didn't know much about gardening, so she also
bought a book that promised to teach garden-challenged
people to grow beautiful flowers. She just wanted to
know enough not to kill the jewel-colored blooms.

For an hour, she worked steadily, digging holes, plant-
ing flowers, laying mulch. The sun blasted down on her,
making her feel as if her blood was boiling. Didn't help
that there was no breeze at all and the oaks in her yard
were busily shading the area where she wasn't.

She liked knowing she was continuing to make her
house beautiful. But the downside to gardening was you
had too much time to think. Naturally, her thoughts kept
spinning back to the man who held her heart and didn't
want it.

"Way to go, Andi," she muttered, patting the dirt in
around a bright red petunia. "You're doing great on the
not-thinking-about-Mac thing."

Disgusted with herself, she sat back on her heels to
admire her work and gave a small sigh of satisfaction.
The flowers were red, white and blue, and with the red
mulch it looked patriotic and fresh and beautiful. Now
all she had to do was find some other chore around the
house to keep her busy. Gathering up her tools and the
empty bags of mulch, she stood up and wished for a moment or two that she had a pool to jump into.

Her cutoff jeans shorts were filthy, her white tank top was sticking to her skin and her ponytail was slipping free, with tendrils of hair hanging down on either side of her face. She wanted a shower, a glass of wine and maybe to lie prostrate on the cool, tiled floor of her kitchen while the air conditioner blew directly onto her.

She might have wished she was out at the ranch with Mac, maybe swimming in the pond behind the house. Skinny-dipping would have been fun on a hot summer day. But that wasn't going to happen, so she let it go on a sigh. Carrying all of her things into the garage, she heard a truck pull into her driveway. The thought of having to be polite and welcoming to a visitor right now made her tired.

Andi wanted some time alone. Time to sulk and brood and enjoy a little self-pity with her glass of cold white wine. So, if it was Vi or Jolene, she'd send them home. The two women had been tag teaming her lately, each of them taking turns to check in with Andi and make sure she wasn't lonely. Well, she *needed* a little lonely at the moment.

With her arguments ready, she came around the corner of the house and stopped dead. Mac. His huge black truck sat in the drive, sunlight glinting off the chrome. The man himself was walking toward her house, looking so good Andi wanted to bolt back into the garage and close the door after her.

She looked *hideous*. Why did he finally decide to come to her when she was hot and sweaty and covered in garden dirt? Quickly, she gathered up her hair, tightened the ponytail, checked out her reflection in the side mirror of her car and brushed spots of dirt off her cheeks. She wasn't wearing makeup because her thought that morning had been, *who needed mascara to plant flowers?* So getting rid of the dirt on her face was really the best she could do and wasn't that all kinds of sad?

She closed her eyes and took a breath. Why had he come here? Was this just another attempt to get her back to the office? Well, she thought, why else would he have come? The man didn't like to lose; Andi knew that better than most. So he'd come back to try to convince her. Again.

Steeling herself for another argument with him, Andi walked out to meet him.

He gave her that wide, slow grin when he saw her and Andi's heart jumped in response. The man would always have that effect on her, she knew. It just wasn't fair that he could score a direct hit on her heart without even trying.

"Flowers are nice," he said.

"Thanks." She tucked her hands into her shorts pockets. To resist the urge to reach for him? Probably. "What're you doing here, Mac?"

"We have to talk." His expression unreadable, Andi thought about it for a few seconds, then nodded. If this really did turn out to be a futile attempt to get her back to the office, it would be better to deal with it. To finally and at last make him see that she wasn't going back. No matter what.

"Okay, fine. Come inside, though. It's too hot out here. And I need something cold to drink."

"Should you be outside working in the heat that way?"

She tossed a quizzical glance at him over her shoulder. "The flower beds are outside, Mac. Hard to plant from the living room."

"I'm just saying, you should be more careful."

Well, that was weird. She headed down the hall toward the kitchen, with Mac right behind her. Andi went straight to the fridge and opened it, relishing the rush of cold air that swept out to greet her. "Tea? Beer?"

"No beer. I'm driving. Listen, Andi—"

"I'm going to stop you right there, Mac. If this is about the office, you can save your breath." She poured two glasses of tea and handed him one. After she took a long drink of her own, she said, "I'm not going over the same old ground again just because you can't accept no for an answer."

"It's not that." He set his tea down, then plucked her glass from her hand and set it aside, too.

The air in the room was cool, but he was standing so near to her that Andi felt the heat of him reach out for her. She'd wished to see him again, but now that he was here, it was painful to be so close to him and yet still so far away.

"Why are you here, Mac?"

He dropped both hands onto her shoulders, looked down into her eyes and said, "It's time you married me."

"What?" This was the last thing she'd expected. A proposal? Granted, not the most romantic proposal in the world, but that didn't matter so much. Demanding she marry him was very Mac after all. But the fact that he was proposing at all was so stunning, Andi felt shaken. Was it possible that he really meant it? Were her dreams about to come true?

He let go of her long enough to dip one hand into his jacket pocket and come up with a small, square ring box. He snapped open the deep red velvet to reveal a round cut diamond so big that when the sunlight caught it, the glare almost blinded her.

She slapped one hand to her chest as if she were try-ing to keep her heart where it belonged. Slowly, she lifted her gaze from the ring to Mac's eyes.

"Marry me, Andi," he urged, eyes bright, deter-mination stamped on his features. "Right away. We can do it this weekend, if you want. I'll call the mayor, he'll fix us up with a license and it'll be all taken care of."

"This weekend?"

He leaned in and planted a fast, hungry kiss on her mouth. "I think that's best. Look, I don't know why you haven't told me yet, but you should know that Violet spoiled the surprise. She told me about the baby."

Andi's mind went blank. She stared at him and tried to get past the knot of emotion lodged in her throat. For a second or two, she couldn't even draw a breath. *Of course.* This was why he'd proposed to her and was insisting on a hurried wedding. It wasn't about love at all. He hadn't had an epiphany. Hadn't realized that she was what he wanted. Mac was only doing what he would consider his "duty."

"No." Andi pushed away from him and took a step backward for extra measure. "Violet lied. There's no baby. I'm not pregnant, Mac."

He looked as though someone had punched him in the stomach. "Why would she lie?"

"I don't know." Andi threw both hands up and let them fall again. Sorrow fought with anger and the sor-row won. Logically, she knew her friend, Mac's sister, had done all of this to bring the two of them together. But emotionally, she had to wonder what Vi had been thinking to play games like this with people's hearts. "She's a romantic," Andi finally said, her voice soft and tinged with a sigh. "She wants us together and probably thought that this was a sure way to make that happen. And I'm sorry but I may have to kill her."

"Get in line," he grumbled, staring down at the ring in his hand before snapping the box closed with what sounded like permanence.

Her heart aching, tears she refused to allow to fall burning her eyes, Andi whispered brokenly, "The point is, I'm not pregnant. At least I don't think so—"

His head came up and his gaze pinned her.

"—but even if it turns out I am," Andi qualified, lifting one hand for emphasis, "that doesn't mean I would marry you just because of a baby. I'm capable of raising a child on my own and I won't get married unless it's for love."

And that was never going to happen, she thought, at least not with Mac. Why was the one man she wanted also the one man she couldn't have? Spinning around, she stomped to the kitchen window, then spun back.

Furious with Violet, Andi blinked hard to keep those tears choking her at bay. For one all-too-brief moment, she'd thought that Mac had come to her because he wanted her. Instead, they were both being dragged over the coals again. And there was just no reason for it.

"Just take the diamond and go, Mac." *Please go*, she prayed silently. Before she cried.

He opened the jeweler's box, looked down at the ring, shining so brightly on its bed of red velvet, and he shook his head. "No." Shifting his gaze to her, he started toward her with long, slow steps.

Andi groaned, and naturally backed up until she hit the wall. Then she had no choice but to hold her ground and try to keep it together until he left again. *Please let that be soon.*

"I'm not going anywhere." His gaze moved over her face, her hair, her mouth, then settled on her eyes again. "When you just said there was no baby, you know what I felt?"

She huffed out a breath, then firmed her bottom lip when it trembled. "Relief?"

He shook his head. "Disappointment."

Andi blinked at him and apparently he read the surprise on her face.

"Yeah, caught me off guard, too." He laughed softly to himself. "Trust me when I say that my little sister and I are going to be having a talk about this."

"Get in line." She repeated his earlier words and he grinned.

"But," he added, moving in on her, crowding her until she couldn't draw a breath without his scent surrounding her, invading her, "it's because of Vi that I'm here. It's just the push I needed, though I doubt I'll be admitting that much to her. Being here with you, thinking about us being married and having a family, made me realize something important."

Andi swallowed hard and whispered, "What's that?"

"It wasn't a baby that had me proposing, Andi. It was *you*." He smiled, stroked her hair back from her face with the tips of his fingers. "A pregnancy gave me the excuse I thought I needed to come here again. To look at you and admit to both of us that it's you I want, Andi. You I need."

"Mac…" Thank God her back was against a wall. Otherwise, her liquefied knees just might have her slumping onto the floor.

"Not done," he said, winking. "I love you, Andi, and I'm just as surprised by that statement as I see you are."

His expression went tender, soft, as he tipped her chin up with his finger to close her mouth. "The thing is, I've counted on you being a part of my life for so long, I never noticed that you had *become* my life."

A single tear escaped and slid along her cheek. He kissed it away.

"Without you, nothing's fun anymore," he whispered, gaze roaming over her features, voice thick. "Not work. Not relaxation. Not the ranch or a damn picnic or anything. I need you, Andi, and more than that, I need you to believe me."

"Mac, I want to. I really do. More than anything." Her heart in her throat, blood rushing through her veins, she couldn't look away from those green eyes of his.

"Then do it." He cupped her face in his palms. "I'm mad at Vi, but I'm grateful to her, too. Her lie gave me the push to come here. To find my life. To do what I should have done years ago."

Confused, shaken, so touched she could hardly see through the blur of those sneaky tears in her eyes, Andi could only watch as he dropped to one knee in front of her.

"Since I'm only doing this once in my life, I'm going to do it right." He took her hand, slid the ring onto her finger and kissed it. Then looking up at her, he said, "I love you, Andrea Beaumont. Maybe I always have. I know I always will. And if you're not pregnant now, I hope you are soon. I want a houseful of kids running around the ranch."

Her free hand covering her mouth, Andi looked down at him and nodded, unable to speak past the growing knot of emotion clogging her throat.

"I'm taking that as a yes."

"Yes." Slowly, Andi sank to her knees beside him. "I love you, too, Mac. So yes, I'll marry you and have babies with you and ride horses and have picnics—"

"And sweaty Easter eggs?" he asked, his smile shining in his beautiful eyes.

Andi threw her head back and laughed. "God, yes. Sweaty Easter eggs."

"And you'll explain that to me at some point, right? Been driving me crazy trying to figure it out."

She laughed again and felt the easing of hurt and disappointment and regret as all of the negative emotions drained away leaving behind nothing but hope. And joy.

"I promise."

"Come home with me, Andi."

"I will." She looked around her shiny new kitchen and knew she'd miss it. Though Mac's ranch house was wonderful and she knew the life they would build there would be amazing, there would always be a place in her heart for this tiny house. Because it was this place that had brought her and Mac together. The hours they'd spent working on it were memories she'd never part with.

As if reading her mind, Mac whispered, "Let's keep this house. You can use it as an escape route the next time I make you mad. Then I'll always know where to find you so I can come get you and bring you home again."

How lovely to have a man know her so well and love her, anyway. Yes, there would be times they'd fight, argue, and she might storm off and come here. Where she would wait for him to come after her to take her home. *Home.* A home and a family with Mac.

"That sounds just right," she said. Then drawing her head back, she looked up at him and asked, "So, is this another rescue?"

"Yeah," he said softly, wrapping his arms tightly around her. "But this time, *you* rescued *me*."

And he kissed her to seal the promise of their future.

Epilogue

Five months later

A Christmas party at the Texas Cattleman's Club was not to be missed. It looked as though half the town of Royal was gathered to celebrate.

There were five Christmas trees, decorated with multicolored lights and ornaments gathered and collected over the years, placed around the room and at the entrance to the club. Strings of tiny white lights were draped along the walls, and the scattering of tables were covered in red and green cloths. Pine boughs jutted up from vases and lay across the tops of framed paintings, with silvery threads of tinsel hanging from them, catching the light and dazzling the eye. Christmas carols were piped through the overhead speakers and champagne flowed like water.

"You're late," Violet said, coming up to Andi for a hug.

"We're always late now." Andi rubbed her belly and gave a small, sweet smile. Turned out Violet hadn't been lying when she'd sent Mac to Andi all those months ago. Of course, she hadn't known it at the time. It had been a wild guess—although Vi liked to pretend she'd had a psychic moment of intuition. Their baby girl would be born in three months and Andi woke every morning grateful for the love in her life.

"The baby's not here yet. It's not her fault," Violet said, threading her arm through Andi's to steer her through the crowd.

"But we start talking about her and making plans and today we were painting her room," Andi admitted wryly.

"Again? I thought you were sticking with the soft peach."

"I was, but it just seemed as though it would feel hot in there in summer," Andi confessed, "so Mac's painting it that pale green it was before."

Violet laughed. "It's so good to see Mac getting all twisted up over his yet-to-be-born daughter."

"Yes," Andi said, "because Rafe is so la-di-da over your son."

Vi grinned. "I have new pictures to show you of your baby's cousin." She sighed and slapped one hand to her heart. "I swear, I never suspected you could love this much. But Rafe and I are so crazy about our baby boy, we're already talking about expanding the family."

"Good," Andi said, chuckling, "because Mac still has plans to fill every bedroom in the ranch house."

Vi blinked. "There are eight of them."

"I know." Andi sighed. "Isn't it great?"

"Hey, there you are." Mac came up behind Andi, put his arms around her and let his hands come to rest on the swell of their child. He was always touching her, touching their baby. It was as if he couldn't stand to be away from her, and Andi was loving every minute of it.

"I missed you. How you doing? Tired? You want anything?"

"Not tired," she said, "but water would be great, thank you." He kissed the side of her neck, winked at Vi, then headed for the bar.

"I'm so happy for you guys," Violet said on a sigh. "I've never seen Mac so relaxed, so…well, happy."

"I am, too." Andi took a deep breath of the pine-scented air and added, "My life is officially perfect."

She had Mac, their baby, their families and friends. Life was just *wonderful*. Looking around the room, Andi let her gaze sweep across the friends and neighbors gathered there. Case and Mellie Baxter looked amazing. She knew Case was planning on running for another term as club president, and Mellie and Andi had made an informal agreement to use their respective businesses to support each other. With Mellie's Keep N Clean, a house-sitting/cleaning business, and Andi's own Put-It-Away, they would each benefit. Andi could pick up new clients and then could recommend Keep N Clean to her customers to help their newly organized homes stay that way.

"It's pretty amazing what Mellie did for the TCC."

"Generous, for sure," Andi agreed. The TCC had decided it wanted to own the land it sat on instead of keeping the long-term lease they already had going with Mellie's family. So they'd officially made an offer for the property. Which she had promptly turned down. Then, with the agreement of her father, who was now back from rehab and doing much better, Mellie had gone ahead and made a gift of the land to the club.

So, this party was not just for Christmas, but a celebration for the Texas Cattleman's Club.

And the party was a huge success. With Christmas only two weeks away, everyone was feeling festive. Nolan and Raina Dane were laughing with the sheriff and his wife, Amanda.

Liam and Hadley Wade were married now and expecting twins, which explained why Liam was plopping Harper down into a chair in spite of her protests.

"What's the smile for?" Violet asked.

"Just thinking about all that's happened to our friends and the town in the last several months."

Nodding, Vi looked around, too. "It was crazy a lot of the time, but I think we all came through really well. Oh, look. There's Jolene and Tom!"

Tom veered off for the bar, clearly a man on a mission, and Jolene headed straight for Vi and Andi. Newly svelte, now that her fourth child and second son had been born a few months ago, Jolene looked as happy as Andi felt.

"Hi, you guys. Isn't this party amazing?" She turned her head to take in her sister. "Andi, you look gorgeous. Love the color red on you."

Andi sneaked a quick look to where Mac, Rafe and Tom were all balancing drinks and talking. "Mac likes me in red. Says it reminds him of what I wore on our first date. He surprised me with the dress this afternoon."

And then he'd taken her to bed and proved to her beyond a shadow of a doubt how beautiful he thought she was. Such a gift, she told herself, to have a man's love, to know that he felt what you did. To *know* that he would always be there for you and your children.

As if sensing her thoughts, Mac turned, looked directly at her and winked.

"Aren't our men just gorgeous?" Vi sighed a little and waved to her husband as Rafe smiled at her.

"Oh, yeah," Jolene agreed with a wink of her own for Tom.

Mac had supported her idea for a business of her own. Put-It-Away was building quickly, and Andi had as many clients as she wanted. She was picky, though, refusing to be drawn into another all-work, no-play scenario. Mac, too, had cut back on time at the office, leaving Tim more and more in charge as Mac himself concentrated on their growing family and the ranch that was the center of their lives.

"Look," Andi said, "there's Kyle and Grace Wade. They look great, don't they? Grace tells me the twins are doing so well that Maddie is quickly catching up to Maggie development-wise."

"I know. It's great." Vi nodded toward the far side of the room. "Oh, Parker Reese and Claire just came in. They're so busy planning their wedding, I've hardly seen Claire lately."

"I was sorry to hear Rafe's sister and her husband wouldn't be able to come for Christmas," Jolene said.

"Me, too," Vi murmured. "But with Nasira pregnant, Sebastian has decreed no long flights."

Jolene frowned. "Is everything all right?"

"Everything's great, but Sebastian is being as protective and proud as Mac is of our Andi. And though Nasira really wanted to be here, I think she's enjoying having Sebastian hover and take care of her."

"Well, we all like that," Jolene said, "whether we cry feminist or not."

"True." Andi turned to smile at her husband as the three men rejoined the women. Mac dropped one arm around her and pulled her into his side.

"Having a good time?"

"The best," she said, smiling up into his eyes.

"Have I mentioned lately how much I love you?"

"I believe you have but feel free to repeat yourself," Andi said, a smile twitching at her lips.

"Have Yourself a Merry Little Christmas" piped from the speakers overhead, and as his arms came around her, she knew that every Christmas from now on would be perfect.

"I think we should go home early," Mac whispered, his mouth so close to her ear that his breath brushed warmly against her skin. "Decorate the tree in our bedroom and then make love in front of the fire."

She smiled as her insides tightened. Leaning into him, she turned her head so she could look out over the crowd while enjoying this private moment.

"I think that's a wonderful idea, Mac."

He tipped her face up and gave her a quick, soft kiss. "Merry Christmas, Andi."

"Merry Christmas, Mac." She leaned into him and smiled as her heart filled with the kind of joy that would be with her forever.

* * * * *

Don't miss a single installment of

TEXAS CATTLEMAN'S CLUB:
LIES AND LULLABIES
*Baby secrets and a scheming sheikh
rock Royal, Texas*

COURTING THE COWBOY BOSS
by USA TODAY *bestselling author Janice Maynard*

LONE STAR HOLIDAY PROPOSAL
by USA TODAY *bestselling author Yvonne Lindsay*

NANNY MAKES THREE by Cat Schield

THE DOCTOR'S BABY DARE
by USA TODAY *bestselling author Michelle Celmer*

THE SEAL'S SECRET HEIRS
by Kat Cantrell

A SURPRISE FOR THE SHEIKH
by Sarah M. Anderson

IN PURSUIT OF HIS WIFE
by Kristi Gold

A BRIDE FOR THE BOSS
by USA TODAY *bestselling author Maureen Child*

***

*If you're on Twitter, tell us what you think
of Harlequin Desire! #harlequindesire*

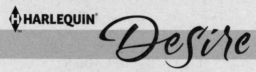

HARLEQUIN®
Desire

Available July 5, 2016

#2455 THE BABY INHERITANCE
Billionaires and Babies • by Maureen Child
When a wealthy divorce attorney unexpectedly inherits a baby, he asks the baby's temporary guardian to become a temporary *nanny*. But living in close quarters means these opposites can't ignore their attraction...by day or by night!

#2456 EXPECTING THE RANCHER'S CHILD
Callahan's Clan • by Sara Orwig
A millionaire rancher bent on revenge clashes with his beautiful employee, who is determined to do the right thing. Their intense attraction complicates everything...and then she becomes pregnant with his baby!

#2457 A LITTLE SURPRISE FOR THE BOSS
by Elizabeth Lane
Terri has worked for—and loved—single father Buck for years, but as the heat between them builds, so does Buck's guilt over a dark secret he's keeping from Terri. And then she discovers a little secret of her own...

#2458 SAYING YES TO THE BOSS
Dynasties: The Newports • by Andrea Laurence
With CEO Carson Newport and his top employee, PR director Georgia Adams, spending long hours together at the office, the line between business and pleasure blurs. But his family's scandals may challenge everything he knows and unravel the affair they've begun...

#2459 HIS STOLEN BRIDE
Chicago Sons • by Barbara Dunlop
For his father, Jackson Rush agrees to save Crista Corday from the con man attempting to marry her and steal her fortune—by kidnapping her from her own wedding! But he didn't count on wanting the bride for himself!

#2460 THE RENEGADE RETURNS
Mill Town Millionaires • by Dani Wade
An injury has forced rebel heir Luke Blackstone back home for rehabilitation...with the woman he scorned years ago. Determined to apologize, and then to seduce the straitlaced nurse, will the man who's made running away a profession stay?

SPECIAL EXCERPT FROM

HARLEQUIN®
Desire

With CEO Carson Newport and his top employee, PR
director Georgia Adams, spending long hours together at
the office, the line between business and pleasure blurs.
But his family's scandals may challenge everything he
knows and unravel the affair they've begun...

Read on for a sneak peek at
SAYING YES TO THE BOSS
the latest installment in the
DYNASTIES: THE NEWPORTS series
by *Andrea Laurence*.

"To the new Cynthia Newport Memorial Hospital for
Children!" Carson said, holding up his glass. "I really can't
believe we're making this happen." Setting down his cup, he
wrapped Georgia in his arms and spun her around.

"Carson!" Georgia squealed and clung to his neck.

When he finally set her back on the ground, both of them
were giggling and giddy from drinking the champagne on
empty stomachs. Georgia stumbled dizzily against his chest
and held on to his shoulders.

"Thank you for finding this," he said.

"I know it's important to you," she said, noting he still
had his arms <u>around</u> her waist. Carson was the leanest of
his brothers, but his grip on her told of hard muscles hidden
beneath his expensive suit.

In that moment, the giggles ceased and they were staring
intently into each other's eyes. Carson's full lips were only
inches from hers. She could feel his warm breath brushing
over her skin. She'd imagined standing like this with him so
many times, and every one of those times, he'd kissed her.

Before she knew what was happening, Carson pressed his lips to hers. The champagne was just strong enough to mute the voices in her head that told her this was a bad idea. Instead she pulled him closer.

He tasted like champagne and spearmint. His touch was gentle yet firm. She could've stayed just like this forever, but eventually, Carson pulled away.

For a moment, Georgia felt light-headed. She didn't know if it was his kiss or the champagne, but she felt as though she would lift right off the ground if she let go. Then she looked up at him.

His green eyes reflected sudden panic. Her emotions came crashing back down to the ground with the reality she saw there. She had just kissed her boss. Her boss! And despite the fact that he had initiated it, he looked just as horrified by the idea.

"Georgia, I…" he started, his voice trailing off. "I didn't mean for that to happen."

With a quick shake of her head, she dismissed his words and took a step back from him. "Don't worry about it," she said. "Excitement and champagne will make people do stupid things every time."

The problem was that it hadn't felt stupid. It had felt amazing.

Don't miss a single story in Dynasties: The Newports
Passion and chaos consume a Chicago real estate empire

SAYING YES TO THE BOSS
by Andrea Laurence, available July 2016!

And
AN HEIR FOR THE BILLIONAIRE by Kat Cantrell
CLAIMED BY THE COWBOY by Sarah M. Anderson
HIS SECRET BABY BOMBSHELL by Jules Bennett
BACK IN THE ENEMY'S BED by Michelle Celmer
THE TEXAN'S ONE NIGHT STAND-OFF by Charlene Sands
Coming soon!

www.Harlequin.com

Whatever You're Into… Passionate Reads

Looking for more passionate reads from Harlequin®?
Fear not! Harlequin® Presents, Harlequin® Desire and
Harlequin® Blaze offer you irresistible romance stories
featuring powerful heroes.

❖HARLEQUIN *Presents*

Do you want alpha males, decadent glamour and jet-set
lifestyles? Step into the sensational, sophisticated world of
Harlequin® Presents, where sinfully tempting heroes ignite a
fierce and wickedly irresistible passion!

❖HARLEQUIN *Desire*

Harlequin® Desire novels are powerful, passionate and
provocative contemporary romances set against a backdrop of
wealth, privilege and sweeping family saga. Alpha heroes with
a soft side meet strong-willed but vulnerable heroines amid a
dramatic world of divided loyalties, high-stakes conflict and
intense emotion.

❖HARLEQUIN *Blaze*

Harlequin® Blaze stories sizzle with strong heroines and
irresistible heroes playing the game of modern love and lust.
They're fun, sexy and always steamy.

Be sure to check out our full selection of books
within each series every month!

www.Harlequin.com